WITHERING

Robert Mathis Kurtz.

SEVEREDPRESS

Copyright © 2012 by Robert Mathis Kurtz.
Copyright © 2012 by Severed Press
www.severedpress.com
Cover design: TCO - www.indie-inside.com
All rights reserved. No part of this book may be reproduced or transmitted in any form or by any electronic or mechanical means, including photocopying, recording or by any information and retrieval system, without the written permission of the publisher and author, except where permitted by law.
This novel is a work of fiction. Names, characters, places and incidents are the product of the author's imagination, or are used fictitiously. Any resemblance to actual events, locales or persons, living or dead, is purely coincidental.
ISBN: 978-1480042223
All rights reserved.

AUGUST:

On days like this, there was only one place Addie Lacher could go to escape the heat, and that was in the shelter of her front porch. It wasn't much cooler there, but it was shaded enough to take the edge off the sun's rage, and she could sit in her ancient rocker (it was older even than she), lean back on the faded orange cushion her husband had bought her and which she had patched so many times that hardly any of the original material remained. That's not much for a ninety-three year old woman, but it was enough for her. She sat, rocked, sipped at the glass of water she had brought, biding her time.

Addie was surprised, but not horrified, when the dead man came up the dusty path toward her porch.

It wasn't the first time such had happened to her. Addie had a talent--*a gift* one of her pastors had called it--and there had been times in her life when the dead were as visible to her as the pages of a book in someone's hands. When she had been a little girl, she had seen her dead grandmother coming out of the negro cemetery near downtown Woodvine. After his mortal stroke she had talked to her dead husband. Still, she had never seen a stranger appear thus, but she was not afraid of him. She knew he couldn't hurt her.

He was quite dark skinned; but she could see that he wasn't black; at least he wasn't black like she was. His skin was more like copper, his hair straight and as the color of tar. He wasn't like any man she had ever seen, and his clothes were strange, too.

The shirt that he wore was white, probably cotton, and she could see through it, could see his wiry body underneath as he drew close in the bright sunlight. His pants were khaki colored, thin, and his shoes were more like slippers. There was a great splotch of red in the front of his shirt, just above his abdomen and below his left nipple. As he climbed the steps to her porch and turned to seat himself in the straight backed chair beside her, she could see a smaller hole in the back of his shirt where the bullet had entered. So, someone had shot him in the back.

"Who are you," she asked him as soon as he was seated. The chair did not creak beneath his weight.

The dead man answered her, but Addie could not understand his name, would not be able to repeat it if someone asked her. It was a strange, foreign name, and Addie knew that he was from far away, that he had not ever lived in Woodvine. He had only died here.

"Why are you here?" Nearby, a flock of crows flew up from the big pine they had roosted in moments before. With hardly a caw, the entire group took wing and made their ways northward, toward Martinsville. A small cloud of sparrows followed in their wake.

"He's overdoing it," the little man said. When he said 'overdoing' it sounded strange, and she had trouble understanding him. Addie finally heard him, though.

"What do you mean?" The air was still, and quite hot.

"It takes much to call up such a thing. And more than what is visible is released." There was concern on the dead man's face.

"I don't understand what you mean," she told him.

That didn't seem to matter to him. "If he doesn't stop, something..." Here, he paused, looking at Addie, sizing her up, seeing her. "Something very big will happen."

"I don't understand what you are saying. I don't understand, and I don't know why you're telling me." Addie leaned forward, looking into his sad brown eyes.

"There is no one else to tell. You have to stop him."

"Stop who?"

"The white man. The bad white man."

That didn't narrow it down much. "I'm sorry, but you don't make much sense," she told him. "What is he doing?"

"He's calling something that kills. Recently, it has only taken animals, but he wants it to kill people. He's done it before...a man who got in his way, children." There was pain beyond physical in his eyes.

"What children?"

"Three of them. Little black children. A long time ago."

Addie knew what he meant then, could still see the faces of Roy and William and Esther Washington. It had been more than twenty years since they'd disappeared, and she still thought about them frequently. "What happened to them? Where are they?"

"You just have to stop him. That's all." There was a sick look on his face. He seemed to be straining.

"Who? Who do I stop?"

But he was gone, nothing more than a strange memory. Addie could see the forest that stood beyond where he had sat. Merely that and nothing more.

After a while, after she felt stronger, she roused herself from where she sat, going to her kitchen so that she could prepare her supper. Nathan Watts would come from Martinsville to see about her in the morning, would probably try to talk her into moving into town where she'd be around people who could see to her day to day welfare instead of having someone come out to her place in the country to check on her one day a week. And once more she would thank him for the generous offer. But she knew that she wouldn't mention what had happened to her. In her life, there had only been a few people she had told when such things had occurred, and all of those people were gone, now. No, she would merely dwell on what she had seen and heard, would try to make sense of it on her own.

That was what she had always done in the past, and it was what she would do now.

Standing before the enameled electric stove with which the congregation had recently gifted her, she wondered what her dreams would bring her tonight. Something would come in them. She was sure of it.

CHAPTER ONE

Going south from the great city of Atlanta, the steel and concrete spreading outward like some gigantic and consuming cancer, one comes, eventually, to Macon; smaller, less of concrete and steel than of hills and trees and slowly rolling rivers. South of there, you come to the even smaller town of Perry, merely a place along the road to Florida and nothing else. Past that town, you can see little besides the endless stands of green and healthy pines that have been planted everywhere by the paper companies that own most of the acreage where towns and farms break the green monotony. Here, the gentle hills of the Piedmont give way to the flat, featureless expanses of the coastal plains: sandy barrens fit for growths of slash pines and little else.

It is there, if you have a reason to leave the safe and modern Interstate, that Highway 27 can be found, nothing save a couple of the usual service stations and the obligatory Stuckey's Restaurant marking the exit. A sign informs those bothering to look that Martinsville lies six miles to the south, along 27.

There is probably no reason for most to go there, but if you did, you would find nothing more than a small city of less than 10,000 people and the typical things to be expected in such a small and isolated county seat.

Beyond there, 27 leads off into piney wastelands visited only by workers on flatbed trucks going to harvest the scaly pines destined for the vats of pulp from which paper is made. About eighteen miles south of Martinsville, there is another, poorly marked road badly in need of repair and leading even further into the sandy barrens where only pines and scrubby oaks rear above the featureless earth. Four miles down the pocked tar and gravel roadway that is labeled Spur 27 by the faded black on white signs on the weed-choked shoulders there is a single-lane bridge of rusting steel and splintering wood that sits, spanning an unmarked and sluggish tributary which the locals know as Fanner's Creek.

After that if your vehicle does not exceed the three-ton capacity of the bridge (or if you feel lucky that day) one can drive for five more potholed miles and come suddenly upon houses standing amidst brown lawns, and water oaks growing in the hot sun. If you were to continue on, and not there turn abruptly about and head back the way you came, you would come to a weather-beaten sign sitting beside this Spur 27. WOODVINE, GA., it reads. Past that sign you could see the remains of a sick and fading village.

A death can be a sad thing, especially if it is a long and lingering one. Sometimes it's better if the blow comes quickly, decisively, and the pain is minimal, the suffering insubstantial.

But how does a town die?

Davis Ryan took his old truck down the sandy road that led toward Billy Wishon's farm. Wishon had shown up at Ryan's house the day before saying that he was having some problems and was wondering if Davis could come out and have a look. Rows of tall, thin slash pines whizzed past as he took the battered Chevy to Wishon's farm; he left great, sandy-dirty clouds billowing behind in the dry summer air. In recent years, whenever there was a problem of just about any kind, the locals would go to Davis and request his help. Davis reckoned he was what served as the 'chief of police' in place of long faded constabulary. He smiled sadly.

It had been a while since he had been out here, east of dying Woodvine, and he'd forgotten how long this particular road really was. Wincing, he had to slow when he hit a patch of hardpan washboard, the rain-rippled ground putting a strain on his worn shocks. He peered with squinting eyes at the close stands of pines, trying to see through them toward the place the natives knew as Thirty Acre Rock--it was a huge expanse of exposed granite that numbered well in excess of a mere thirty acres and, from what he understood, was responsible for the poor rate of growth of the surrounding pine forests. In a way, he thought, all of that barren rock was partly responsible for the slow death of Woodvine.

Stahl's Lumber Yard had once been the main employer in town, but with the local timber good for little besides the anemic stands of slash pines and pulpwood, the mill had picked up and had moved twenty miles to the north, to Martinsville. And so it went.

Driving free of the washboard, Davis sped up again, pulling away from the drifting cloud of sand that threatened to swallow him. He gave up trying to look for a patch of Thirty Acre Rock. He never had liked that place, despite the fact that some folk actually had been known to picnic there in years past, and there had even been some talk of making it a state park; but that had been from desperate men clutching at straws toward the end.

Stillman's Branch intersected the huge expanse of rock, and he recalled that in days gone the kids had liked to go there to swim on hot summer days. He had tried it once, but the walk out to the stream had been a sweltering one, and the journey back had sapped what pleasure he had derived from the short dip he had taken there. The place had always given him the creeps, and he hadn't been back in years. Damn. How many years had it been?

Although he hated to think of how far Woodvine had fallen, he had to smile and chuckle to himself there in the hot cab of his truck. Old Billy Wishon had taken the time and effort to drive out to his house to ask for help because, as he had put it, he had needed "a young feller" to look over his problem. Davis was sixty years old, and it was funny to consider so many others thinking of him as a "young feller". But the smile quickly faded as he recalled that he truly was the youngest man yet living in Woodvine. How far down the town had drifted!

Ahead, appearing at a distance aside the arrow straight road, he could see a battered, black mailbox atop a worn and splintering post. There was a turnout where the occasional mailman could reverse direction and head back to humanity.

Beyond that, the road vanished in a tangle of choking weeds, sickly trees, and Spanish bayonet; past that, rows of slash pine went on and on. Davis found the drive that led down to the Wishon farm and turned there. Clouds of dark, soft sand settled to earth behind him.

In a short moment he came out of the vegetation that grew so close about the driveway and arrived on the big lawn that preceded the Wishon home. The grass was brown and rather dying; patches of sand showed through the sick yard. Wishon's truck was sitting and baking in a bare place and Davis parked next to it and shut down his own truck. He got out, feeling the wet heat of the day pressing down on him. *Jesus*. There was a familiar creaking sound and Davis looked toward the long, tin-roofed porch of the frame house to see old Billy stepping out. The farmer was wearing his requisite overalls, his red cotton shirt sleeves rolled up to reveal tanned arms lean and muscled despite his years. Worn boots thumped atop dry planks and the old man raised his pipe in greeting.

"Davis," he hailed. "I didn't expect you out quite this early, but we sure are glad to see you." Behind him, his wife was emerging from the shadows of the house. She wiped at her brow with the corner of her apron, the slight smile there doing little to hide the concern and worry on her face.

"Hello, Shelley," Davis said, waving at Billy's wife. The expression she wore bothered him. She seemed, at a glance, genuinely frightened. He wondered if perhaps they were having problems with some of the rowdy kids from Martinsville. There had been times when they had vandals roaming into Woodvine. But that had been years ago, when the town had first shut down its courthouse annex and police station, when the storefronts on Main Street had initially emptied out and the buildings had proven juicy targets for bored children from the more prosperous county seat.

Even then, though, the problems had been with the remaining citizens close to town, never the ones out here on the fringes. He came up to their porch, rubbing a sleeve across his forehead.

"Hello, Davis." She smiled at him, trying to hide her concern. "Would you like to come in and have a cool drink before y'all head out to the pasture?"

"Yes, ma'am, I would." She turned and Billy held the screen for him as he entered the front of the house. It was cooler there; a large, black fan blew air at them from its post atop an old oak table. Slowly, the fan oscillated, stopped, turned back on its half revolution.

"I hope tea is okay with you. I'd have you some lemonade, but

I haven't been over to Martinsville in two weeks, and I just don't have any lemons. And I cain't stand that powdered stuff. If we cain't have the real thing, then I can just plain do without."

"Yes, ma'am, I know how you feel, and tea is fine with me."

Actually, Davis rather liked the Kool-Aid brand of lemonade, and he usually kept a pitcher of the tart, sugary drink in his refrigerator. He followed Mrs. Wishon past the front room and its antiques, down the long, bare hallway, into the kitchen at the very rear of the house. When Mr. Wishon entered, the two men sat at the worn table against the east wall and waited while Shelley poured and served the tea. There was a pleasant sound of ice clinking against glass, hinting of cool days to come. Davis raised a converted jelly jar to his lips and took a long swallow of the sweet beverage--Mr. Wishon liked his sugar, it seemed.

After a slug of the tea, Davis put his glass down and regarded the two pair of eyes that stared at him. Even old Billy looked worried, and that was something he hadn't noticed when the old fellow had stopped by his home, asking him to come out, then hustling back to his truck for the return home. Davis felt bad that he had made the man wait a day before he had come. He realized now that Billy had been hurrying back home, neither wanting his frail wife out in the heat of day, nor wanting to leave her alone at home for too long. In the shadowy kitchen, Mrs. Wishon looked every day of her eighty-four years.

"Well, Billy, what seems to be the problem? You didn't make it too clear when you came by the house yesterday." He touched his tea glass but did not lift it to his lips. Condensation crept around his hard fingers.

"I ain't quite sure what kind of problem I got, Davis." The farmer and his wife sat, blinked.

"What do you mean?" Davis felt a trickle of sweat tickling beneath his armpit, sliding down his ribs.

"Something killed a couple of my cows." He said it. His wife looked up at him.

"What? Some kids from Martinsville out firing a shotgun?"

"No, nothin' like that. Not people, I don't think."

"Some wild dogs? You know how we had some problems with wild dogs back in '83." Davis took a draw on the tea.

"No, I don't think it's no wild dogs." Wishon added nothing.

"A bear, then?"

"Yeah. Could be. Can you come and take a look with me?" The farmer stood, not waiting for Davis' reaction.

"Sure. Just lead the way and we'll have a look." He noticed how the concern seemed to intensify in Shelley's eyes. Her hand reached out and touched Billy's.

"Don't worry, Momma, I'm gonna take my shotgun with us. I just want to take Davis out there and show him around for a few minutes. We'll be alright." He clumped over to the corner, and for the first time Davis noticed the pair of twelve gauges leaning in a corner near the back door. "Here, Davis. You take this one." He handed one of the weapons to Ryan.

"Well, if you..." He saw the expressions on the couple's faces, the fear. "Sure, Billy. I'll take it." Wishon pushed the door open, and he preceded the other out onto the back porch, down the stairs and into the yard which was as dry and brown there as in the front.

"You just wait here, Momma. We'll be back in a few minutes."

Billy's wife said nothing and merely watched as the two men passed by the chicken coops full of the pale, laconic birds. They soon vanished in the long rows of green corn that stood tall about them despite the paucity of rain the countryside had been experiencing.

"Y'r corn looks good, Billy. Better 'n some I've seen." Davis tried to make small talk, to take the edge off the tension he was feeling, that he knew Billy was feeling.

"Got me some good thundershowers this season. Yeah, we'll get some corn this summer." He added nothing more. They tread along, Billy leading the way.

"Where we headed, Billy?"

"Back here a ways. I got me my pasture out here past the three acres o' corn I planted this year. Too damn far from th' house."

They came out of the corn and to the fenced edge of a grassy expanse. In the center of the pasture was a drying pond where the cattle could get a drink, could cool themselves when they had to.

On the far side of the pasture Davis could see a pair of low forms, almost like scabs on the surface of the grass. "That them," he asked.

"Yeah. Found 'em day before yesterd'y." The old man clambered quickly over the fence, pulled at a slat and freed it so that Davis could step over with less effort.

"Thanks." The two headed for the other side, Billy eyeing the forests that started on that border.

"Check them woods, Davis. I don't trust 'em these days." The old farmer's gaze was locked on the wall of ugly pines that grew along his pasture, around his entire farm. "I seen things lately."

"I don't see anything, Billy. What're you talking about? You got bear problems?" As they neared the corpses of the pair of animals, Davis could begin to smell the stench of rotting meat.

"Bear? I reckon. I hope." They drew to within twenty feet, avoiding soft dollops of cow shit. The stink from the putrefying animals was intense. Blowflies hummed in the air, angrily feasting. The two men halted.

"God!" Davis stared, seeing up close what he had not realized from the opposite side of the pasture. The pair of milk cows had been completely dismembered. He counted the eight legs lying about in a semi-circle of gore-blackened grass. Heaps of purple, rotting entrails were scattered out from bodies that had been torn open, pinkish ribs jutting brokenly from dripping flesh. One of the cow's heads had been torn from its neck. Already, maggots were swimming in empty eye sockets. Bovine lips seemed to pulse with life; Davis knew why, not wanting to go nearer, but needing to.

"I've never seen anything like this, Billy. It has to be a bear kill, don't it?"

Wishon said nothing. He merely stood and waited while Davis approached the bodies of the dead cows. Ryan took as close a look as he was able under the circumstances. In a few seconds he returned to the old farmer.

"Bear, Billy. Has to be." Wishon looked unconvinced.

"Come here," the farmer said. "I want to show you something else." He headed for a corner of the pasture, the furthest point from his house. Davis followed him.

"What now, Billy?" He tagged along until they got to a corner post where there was a wide sandy spot where no grass grew. The old man stopped and pointed.

"Look there, Davis. What d' you make of that?"

Kneeling, Ryan hunkered down so that he could take a close look. There in the floury sand was a track.

"What d' you make of that," Wishon repeated.

It looked to be a three-toed bird track, but for the fact that it was about two feet in length and eighteen inches across.

The trio of toes spread out in a forty-five degree angle, definite scales embossed in the soft sand. You could see where the points of claws had touched down. Davis stood, his eyes yet locked on the mark in the sand.

"Somebody's playing a joke on us, Billy." Still, a chill went creeping up Davis' back.

"A damned expensive joke." Wishon turned back to the dead cows.

"Maybe so, but you can't think this track is for real. I mean, what the hell is it?"

"I don't know, but it don't look like no bear track."

"What about your dogs? You always keep some good hounds. Wouldn't they kick up a fuss if there was a bear around here?"

"Davis, I ain't seen my hounds since the day before I found these cows. They just disappeared. Fed 'em on Tuesday morning and that's the last I seen of 'em. Gal, Will, and Mark. All three of 'em's gone. I ain't never had my hounds disappear like that!"

"Where did they go?"

"You tell me."

"Billy, I think we need to go over to Martinsville and see the sheriff. If somebody's out here stealin' your hounds, killin' your cattle and playin' damn fool jokes, we need to have him come out and have a look. It must be some spoiled kids from over there."

"I don't know, Davis. I just don't know. There's other things."

"What do you mean?"

The old famer gazed into the woods. "I mean like right now. Listen. What do you hear?"

Davis listened, could hear only his own breath and the incessant buzzing of the blowflies. "Nothing, Billy. What are you getting at?"

"That's what I mean. I've lived out here since I was born, an' I ain't never heard it get quiet like this. Where's the locusts? Where's the birds? I ain't heard a jay or a thrasher in over a week! No crows, even! It's plumb drivin' me an' Shelley crazy!"

"Look, Billy. Don't go all to pieces over this. You and Shelley just sit tight and I'll drive over to Martinsville for you and talk to the sheriff. I'll get him out here so that he can take a look and see what's going on. I'll bet you money that some kids are just messing around here and have been pulling some of the same stuff over his way. You'll see." Davis brushed the sand off of his knees and turned toward the Wishon farm. "Now let's head on back before Shelley wonders what's happened to us."

That last remark seemed to spur Wishon. "Yeah. I don't like leaving her for too long by herself. Come on." They headed back across the pasture, climbed the fence, tromped through the green corn growing high above their heads. They left the blowflies to their feast.

Leaving the shotguns in the kitchen, the three went to the front of the house and then Billy and Davis went to the yard and Davis' waiting truck. Davis turned to the old man before he climbed into the cab of his pickup. "Tell me, Billy. Have you seen anyone out here? I mean, I don't think anyone's going to be messing around at the end of this road without you seein' 'em."

Billy considered for only a moment. "Nope. I ain't seen any strangers out this way." He paused. "But I did see crazy ol' Red out here late last week."

"Red? What was he doing out here?" Davis perked up at the mention of Woodvine's former mayor.

"Hell, I don't know. He was just toolin' around in that old Woodvine Police car. I saw him turnin' around at the end of the road here. He does that every now and again. You know."

"Yeah, I know. Gives me the creeps sometimes the way he drives around in that old squad car. Reminds me how much I used to love this town."

"What town, Davis? I don't think there's enough left of Woodvine to even call a town anymore." The old farmer slapped the hood of Davis' half-ton. "I don't want to keep you," he said.

"Okay, Billy. You and Shelley look for me day after tomorrow.

I'll run over to Martinsville in the morning, and see if I can't get the sheriff over here." He climbed into his truck and started it up.

"Sounds good t' me. We'll see you," he said, being reasonable. But Davis could see the worry in the old man's eyes.

Davis pulled away from the Wishon farm, watching the figure of Billy in his rear view mirror until the old man disappeared behind the billows of soft sand the truck threw up behind it. He thought about the old couple there alone in their secluded house, of the way those cows had been butchered by God knew who.

He thought, too, of crazy old Red Sage, Woodvine's last mayor—its only mayor from '77 until the last election in '88. The way Red drove around in that ancient police car was unnerving; the guy just wasn't all there, it seemed, the death of his town just more than he could take. Davis wondered how many of Woodvine's former and present citizens knew about Red's role in the death of the town? Hell, what did it matter?

As he sped down the lonely road toward the paved spur, Davis couldn't get that strange track out of his mind; but that was just another thought in the jumbled strangeness of the day.

CHAPTER TWO

Leaving the dirt track hemmed in by the close stands of pines, Davis turned left down the old spur road, weaving wide into the opposite lane to avoid a gaping pothole that had not quite finished filling with sand. Returning to the correct lane, Davis drew his lips taut thinking that it would be never when they finally got some of that state money that flowed like a river through Martinsville so that they could have this spur repaved. He knew that it was unlikely Woodvine could generate enough of a fuss to make the politicians at the county seat let go of any of their cash. Woodvine just didn't have what it took; they just weren't worth the effort to be noticed. It hadn't always been that way.

Shifting gear, Davis remembered how Woodvine had been in his youth. There had been a lot more people then—the population had once topped 4,500. And there had been things to do in his town, reasons to stay and live. Stahl's Lumber Yard had employed almost two hundred people before it had begun to downgrade the operation in Woodvine so that they could concentrate on their new yards in Martinsville (of course).

Thinking back, he reckoned that one movement of jobs had been the last, killing stroke. It wasn't three years after that the high school had closed its doors, and even the town's two elementary schools had followed suit within another couple of years. There just weren't any children left with all of the young blood moving away, leaving the town behind.

He passed the side road that led to down to the Georgia Power substation that brought them one of the few visitors the town got these days. Even so, it had been weeks since one of the trucks from the utility had been around to check on the station; it pretty much ran itself, and would continue to, as long as no one tampered with it.

Ahead, the encroaching forests gave way to the edges of what was Woodvine. He passed Ernie Butler's house and saw the big-bellied man out in his yard loading twigs and yard trash into a wheelbarrow. The other man waved at him, smiling. Davis smiled back and continued on. He passed more houses: Ed and Mary Childers, John and Beth Martin, Mary Gray (living alone since her retarded daughter Virginia had died last August), Wilber and

Eileen Jackson; then he passed a dozen other households, and he knew them all--every single one of them. Davis didn't think there was a person left in town to whom he hadn't spoken in the last six months; he had talked to all one hundred and seventeen of them.

Damned if he wasn't the walking, talking, breathing census of Woodvine. Somebody had to be, because he knew that no one outside the community gave a flying fart.

Then he came upon the sight that never failed to send him spinning down into a vortex of melancholy: old Woodvine, herself.

Her diminutive skyline reared above him as he tooled toward the center of town. There was Benny Pyle's old Chevrolet dealership sitting empty these twenty years. The lot was barely visible bits of concrete and rusted light posts jutting up and seen beneath growths of bear grass and tenacious weeds. Earlier in the summer he had seen Mary Gray picking blackberries in the tangles there. He remembered because he had stopped to warn her about copperheads and canebrake rattlers and she had turned to him with a wistful look and said, "I just remembered how much Virginia loved blackberry cobbler, so I...". Davis had ended up helping her wade into the thorny mess and together they had plucked several gallons of the sweet berries—he recalled the bellyache from eating the entire cobbler the woman had baked for him.

After the old dealership, he came to the row of storefronts that lined either side of Main Street. Bradbury's was an empty husk; milky plate glass barely hid the mannequins that stood pale and naked in the display at the front of the store. He was glad that the elder Mr. Bradbury had not lived to see his son close the place down in '88 and cut his losses to head for Atlanta.

For some reason, the vandals who had hit the storefronts back in '89 had missed Bradbury's; Davis had wondered about that.

Then there was Jack Polites's restaurant. Davis had always gotten a kick out of listening to Mr. Polites speak with that strange union of Greek and southern accents. Yeah, the Greek had lasted right up until the end--up until the county had made the decision to close up Long Creek and Willows Elementary Schools.

That had been the note that had said "give up" to Jack Polites.

Davis had eaten at Jack's the last day it had opened its doors.

"Yah, Davis. My brother in Macon makes fun o' me. Says I'm wastin' my time gettin' poor in Woodvine. Says I should come on up to Macon and help 'im open a new restaurant there. So, 'at's what I'm doin'. You been a good customer to me, Davis. I'm go'n' miss you." And then he'd added, with a wink, "I'm glad I voted for you for mayor back in '84!" But Davis had already known that. He looked away when he passed the boarded up windows of Jack's Place.

After that, there was the branch of the Union Bank, faded blue columns all cracked and whitening from sun and rain and no one to pay them any mind. Maybe old Jack Polites hadn't been all that poor, because Davis had seen the expression on Dan Beach's face when Jack had closed his accounts there. Dan had been the branch manager, and he'd been fighting tooth and nail to keep that branch open; he'd probably been keenly aware that he had been little more than competent at his insignificant, little branch, and he didn't want to fight the sharks that would menace him in anything greater than his puddle environment. Davis had heard that the slight, milquetoast fellow had killed himself with an overdose of sleeping pills not two years after moving to Martinsville to be some kind of assistant at one of the branches there. Poor guy.

Continuing, he came to Millard Lock's Sixty-Six service station.

Here at the beginning of the town square, Davis had formerly bought his gas and had taken his trucks to be serviced. Millard had been a portly type, continuously happy, incessantly working, his hands covered in grease, his cheek bulging with Red Man chewing tobacco. Between his work and his spitting, he usually had a new joke to tell, but Lord knew where he heard them, because he never seemed to leave town. And Davis recalled the constant trickle of Yankee tourists who had once stopped to fill their tanks at Millard's gas station. He remembered the cars, the tags indicating the northern states, the confused expressions on the faces of these Yankees wondering how they had ended up here in *this godforsaken burg we must have made a wrong turn on 27 and we'll just fill up thank Jesus they have a filling station and then we'll get on our frigging ways to Florida soon oh please soon.*

But those Yankees had spent their money there. They had bought their gas, maybe a new fan belt or windshield wiper blades, and perhaps a cold soda from the coke machine and something called a 'moon pie' for the kids. And sometimes they had just gone ahead and eaten at Jack's restaurant and maybe had gone over to Bradbury's to buy those swimming trunks they had forgotten and a pair of flip-flops for the kids to walk on the beach at Panama City with.

And that money had filtered its way into the general economy of Woodvine--not much, but enough so that the lack of it hit like a bomb when the Interstate was opened up twelve miles to the east of Woodvine so that no one (NO ONE) ever (EVER) found themselves down the little side spur of state road 27 on their ways to Florida. Dwelling on that, Davis thought that perhaps that loss had hurt as much as when the Stahl family closed up their lumber mill. He never saw any strange Yankee faces here in Woodvine anymore. You'd have to be terribly, terribly lost to find Woodvine, now.

Going on, he circled around the town square, around the single-story police station and jail built of cinderblock. Then he was passing the courthouse annex, the granite facade no less imposing than in days when the place had been busy with people working. *If only*, Davis thought, *we hadn't lost that bid to become the county seat back in '72. If only we had won that honor, then the jobs of bureaucracy would be ours and that would have been enough to sustain us. We could have pushed through that proposal back in '74 to extend the spur of highway 27 straight through town and on to the impending Interstate; that would have salvaged us at least some of our tourist trade. And then Stahl's Lumber Yard could have remained, and the young people would've had jobs, and Jack Polites would've made money selling meals, and old Mr. Bradbury's kids wouldn't have closed up shop, and Millard would still be pumping gas and telling jokes at his 66 station, and everything would just be so hunky-dory.*

As he rounded the square, he saw the squad car ensconced in its spot in the weed-picked parking lot. That meant that Red Sage was there. He was in the court house probably wandering around, pretending that he was still mayor of a town that wasn't dead. 'The bastard'. Davis slowed down and pulled into the parking lot, stopped his pickup beside the '58 Chevy.

Getting out, he felt again the hot press of summer air. He stood and looked at the aging auto, at the markings not yet faded on the doors and trunk: CAR 302 WOODVINE POLICE DEPT. Why in the hell they had numbered it 302 was beyond Davis. It had been the one and only car the Woodvine Police Department had ever owned.

Perhaps it was to impress those Yankee tourists who had once trickled steadily through town. He wondered why Red insisted on driving around in the damned thing. And how had the bastard ended up with it, anyway? He reckoned it was because no one had been around to say no to him as the town was keeling slowly over. He reckoned, also, that such had always been the problem: no one had ever been able to say no to Red Sage.

Well, if Red was inside the courthouse, then he might just as well go in, also. He went up the wide granite stairs to the big doors. He pulled, and the door was not locked. Inside, all was dark; weak beams of yellow light entered through webbed windows and cracks in nailed-down boards. There was the stink of dry dust and slowly moldering paper. Davis propped the front door open with a bit of broken granite, then he stepped in.

He hadn't been inside the building since the morning after the little shits from Martinsville had ridden through town, shattering the windows of closed up businesses, firing pistols into the sweltering night air, screaming drunkenly, and driving their hot rods onto people's lawns. To his knowledge, none of the kids had ever been caught and punished, although he supposed that some law enforcement official or another had known who the guilty parties were, because the act was never repeated.

Ben Harrison had been sheriff then; it would've been just like Ben to have cornered the punks in some dive or another and he'd probably scared the hell out of them. At any rate, the cleanup he'd helped with had been the only one. The courthouse was just as he recalled it.

Looking down, Davis could see that there was a well-traveled pathway through the thick dust that had gathered on the floor over the years. Red Sage came here from time to time he knew, but from the looks of the way he'd cleared through the dust, it was more often than Davis had guessed. He didn't even need to follow the well-worn trail to know where Red was. Woodvine's old mayor was obviously in his office, that large room at the end of the wing that jutted out from the main building, the wing that had been added onto the courthouse in '74, after the roadwork money for pushing the spur through town had been voted down. The fiasco had been a kind of consolation to the town, a tidbit tossed to them for being such good losers. In reality, it was a nice juicy bone for Woodvine's version of Benedict Arnold; it had all been for...

"Red!" Davis shoved the door open with a thrust of his foot. Woodvine's mayor did not even flinch at the sound, at the loud voice booming at him; he merely turned slowly in his swiveling chair, the spring squeaking for an agonizing moment.

Red looked up from his seat. The sun shone through the window the older man had pried open, spearing him in bright, hot light. He was a bulldog brute, shoulders still broad despite his age, his face set in a jowly frown because of those bitter years. His blond hair had gone to gray, but it was as thick as when he had been a youth of twenty. It would take more than a sixty-year-old man screaming his name to startle him out of his own melancholy. He glared up at Davis. "Well, if it isn't Woodvine's Finest," he said.

"What are you doing in here? Come back to reminisce?" Davis took a step into the office, bare but for the desk and the big, castored chair in which Red was seated.

"This is my office, Ryan. Always has been. Always will be.

Who are you to be asking me what I'm doing here?" There was not a little hatred in the sparkle of his glare.

"Well, it's kind of weird for you to be here, Red." He said it, was glad that he'd said it. "It's crazy for you to be sitting in here just like it's crazy for you to be driving around in that old police car."

"This is my town, Davis. The people of Woodvine always came to me. Always did." There was a smile that had crept somehow to

Red's bulldog face; it was not pleasant to look upon. "You never did whip me in any election, Davis. Neither you nor anyone else, for that matter. The people always came to me. When it mattered."

"And you always fucked them over."

"You watch what you say to me, Davis Ryan. I've still got friends, you know."

"What are you talking about? What friends?"

It almost seemed as if Sage had stopped breathing. He sat immobile in his seat, staring at Davis, gritting his teeth. Davis was wondering if the old man wasn't actually thinking of jumping him.

"You ain't got any friends left in Woodvine, Red. What friends you did have here are either dead or moved away. The only ones left are the ones who know how bad you screwed up Woodvine, and they don't have any use for you." Davis realized that his hands were balled into hard fists, and he did not unclench them.

"You're a liar. I never did any harm to this town. I only tried to help it!" Red's hands were on the arms of his chair, as if he were about to rise.

"We all know about the shit deals with your cronies in Martinsville! We know how you sold us down the river when Woodvine was up to be the county seat. How you traded our votes away for money. How much was it, Red? And we know about how you did the same when that road bond came up for a vote! What did Martinsville get out of the deal? Did they get a new football stadium that some rich bastards could name after their drunken dead sons? Did you get the money for your very own, brand new office? For a courthouse that was gonna be shut down in a few years? And did you keep our businesses goin'? Did you? Huh? What the fuck did you ever do for this town? You ain't done shit for Woodvine!" Davis realized he had advanced a step or two on the former mayor.

Completely unafraid of the younger man, Red aimed himself at Ryan, ready to spring on him. "You're a liar, Davis. I never did any of those things." Some of the strength seemed to have flowed out of Red, as if hearing the truth from someone's mouth had sapped him of energy. "If I were you, I'd keep those lies to myself. I've got friends, Davis, I..."

At that, Red slumped back in his chair with a loud squeak of rusting springs. He was saying something, but Davis could not understand what the mutterings were.

"Red? Are you okay?" Yes, Davis hated the man, held him accountable for the awful things that had been done to Woodvine, but he did not want to see the old bastard die in front of him; and he did not want to feel responsible for causing Red to suffer a heart attack. He stepped toward the other. "Red! Answer me!"

Hands open in his lap, Sage turned his gaze up to Davis who now stood directly before him, close enough to strike, if Red so chose. Most of the rage was gone from his sparkling glare; hate had been replaced by mere contempt.

"You think you're so smart, don't you Davis? I never did anything bad to this town. Everything I did I did for Woodvine, not against it. And you and those others are too quick to count this town out. Not me. I never intended to see this town die like this. And I won't. I won't see it die like some dried up old hound. You mark my words. There's some wonderful times left for Woodvine. Great things!"

If he had ever wondered about Red retaining any sanity, his doubts were now erased. It was plain that the old mayor was as mad as Davis had ever suspected. Any urge the younger man had held to strike at him flowed away, preceding a kind of apathetic pity for him. He forgot the angry words that were yet unsaid. "This town is finished, Red. It died years and years ago. It just ain't been buried yet, that's all." Davis turned and left the room, wanting suddenly to be away from the old and decaying courthouse.

Still in the room that had been his office, Red remained in his former throne, staring into the dark hallway outside his door; staring into dark places beyond that. "Not yet," he said to himself. "This town isn't dead, yet."

He listened to the receding growl of Davis Ryan's pickup truck until it faded away.

CHAPTER THREE

Past the courthouse Davis continued on, bypassing the paved route that would have taken him around the square and back the way he had come. He would have to come back this way, later, when he would make the trek to hated Martinsville, but for now he wanted to go home and relax for a little while. He hated to admit it, but he was feeling a bit tired. Just the heat, he mused.

Beyond the square, the spur road was even more pocked and full of sand-eating potholes than on the rest of its length. This was the side of town where most of Woodvine's remaining residents still lived. Another two dozen or so homes, his own included, and several unpaved roads where a few old farmers continued to eke out a living from their places. And further back than that, he knew old Addie Lacher still lived in her tin-roofed shack far away in the piney woods. He hadn't seen the old black woman in a long time-- it'd been a good two months since he'd checked in on her.

He knew that some of Woodvine's citizens still thought that she was some kind of voodoo witch. He knew better, though; she was just an old woman living alone in the sticks. Davis didn't worry too much about her because the AME Zion church over at the county seat always sent someone to check up on her every week or so.

He passed Rich and Ada Ryerson walking along the road, tooted his horn and waved at them. They waved back and moved aside, walking hand in hand. Ada's blue dress fluttered in the backwash of wind from his passing truck. He thought of Michelle Hearn.

Michelle's house was just ahead, on the right. He knew she would be home--she went once every two weeks into Martinsville to buy groceries, and she'd done that a week ago. He enjoyed her company, always had, and a visit with her would calm him after his encounter with Red Sage. As a matter of fact he and the widow had been kind of *dating* of late, and she had even gone so far as to host his upcoming birthday party.

Spying the bright red mailbox she'd built in the shape of an overgrown birdhouse, he slowed and turned in to her sandy-grassy drive. Shutting down the truck's motor, he sat for a moment and watched the front door of her house, waiting to see if she would come out at the sound of his arriving truck. She couldn't be expecting him, he knew. But she soon appeared at the door, smiling. He smiled back and climbed out.

"Davis!" She held the door for him as he came up the front steps to her porch, his shoes grinding sand on the poured concrete. "I didn't think I'd see you, today. But I'm glad you stopped by!"

"Any reason?" he asked, grinning, but not stooping to kiss her wonderful face.

"No. No particular reason. But you know I'm always glad to see you." She edged aside as he came in, then wiped her hands on her apron. "I've been in the kitchen making up a cake," she told him, explaining the flour on her fingers. Davis at once saw that she was not wearing her wedding band, staring at the pale, indented space on her ring finger. Michelle noticed him staring there.

"I took off the ring while I mixed up the batter," she told him. "I haven't lost it."

"Of course not. I'm sorry I was staring. It's just that I've never seen your hand without it." That wasn't quite true. She hadn't worn a wedding band when they had been children not yet out of high school.

Feeling awkward, she hustled back to the kitchen. "I've got to pour the batter into the pans before it gets any thicker," she explained. "Why don't you just come on back here with me?"

Davis followed her to her bright kitchen, sunlight filling the room through tall windows, ruffled blue curtains tucked aside.

He watched as she went to the central counter and began to pour cake batter into low pans. "A layer cake," he stated.

"Yes." She didn't look back to him.

"Yellow cake?" he asked.

"Yes," still pouring, scraping now with a spatula.

"Wouldn't be making any chocolate icing, would you?"

"As a matter of fact, I am." This time, she looked over and smiled at him.

"Well! What a coincidence. That happens to be my favorite!"

Davis returned the smile, and he thought of how pretty she was.

Yes, her face was lined with age, more wrinkled with time, but he could look into her great blue eyes and recall the girl with whom he had shared affection, and she was as pretty as ever she had been. It was times like this when he knew that he should have married her when he'd had the chance. But there was no going back.

"I can't imagine such a plain and simple cake being anyone's favorite. I really can't. But it's what you like the best, so it's what I'm going to whip up." Finished with the pans, she took them to the oven, adjusting it until she was satisfied.

"Well, I'm a plain and simple man," he stated. "A plain cake with chocolate icing is about as exciting as I can take."

"Is that why you're too stubborn to move away from this town? I have never understood how someone like you could stand to live here in tiny old Woodvine. Even when it was more than a few old people." At that, some of the sparkle fled from her face.

Ignoring that last, Davis kept the conversation going. "What else have you got planned for me, woman?"

"Planned? What are you talking about?"

"Well, my birthday is tomorrow, and I can't imagine why you'd be baking such a plain and simple cake, otherwise. Any surprises?"

"No. No surprises for you, Davis. Just a cake and some familiar company."

Why don't you marry her now, you old fool? Ask her! Davis shifted in his seat, feeling the hard slats of the straight back chair in which he sat. "Michelle," he began.

"Yes?"

You'll screw up everything if you marry her, you idiot!

Think! He cleared his throat, feeling a tightness there, as if the flesh was closing up to prevent the words from coming out.

"I...," he continued.

"What is it, Davis?"

She'll come right on in to your bachelor life and reorganize everything! Was that so bad? Maybe. "I was just wondering if you had invited Pat Wilson over. For tomorrow, I mean."

The tension was gone, now that he'd again avoided asking her. Her back to him, wiping her white countertop clean of flour and batter, she answered. "Yes, Davis, I did invite him over. And he said he'd be coming. "There, are you happy, now?

"Thank you," he said. "You know he's my best friend, and I'd hate to not have him over for this."

"I know that." She turned and smiled at Davis. "That's why I asked him to come." Even though she couldn't stand him because of the things he'd said of her son's sacrifice, of her Tommy giving up his life for his country.

"I know it's hard for you to understand how Pat thinks, about how he thought of that war. He just doesn't see it the way that you do, that's all."

"Well, he should keep his thoughts to himself. He should've seen that there was a reason, a good reason for why Tommy died like he did. God wouldn't just let him die for no good reason, Davis. He wouldn't!" Even after twelve years, the memory of her son's death could bring her to tears. That was something which Davis could not even pretend to understand. He'd always been a selfish bachelor, with no children, no way of knowing what it was like to have a son whose world he could revolve around. But Michelle had, and he tried to understand.

Standing, Davis went to her, placed his arm about her shoulders and pulled her to him. "Let's not think of unhappy things," he said.

"You're right. I won't think about it. I promise." She missed her husband, missed him terribly. Davis felt her stiffen, slightly, beneath his touch.

Hold her, you idiot. Kiss her. Comfort her. "Well,

Michelle, I need to be getting along. I've got to head over to Martinsville to see the sheriff about Billy Wishon's problem."

"Oh, yes! What was that all about? What kind of problem did he have?"

"It's his cattle," Davis told her, his arm falling back to his side. "Somebody, or some critter, killed two of his cows.

Plus, his hounds are missing. I think it's some mischief from some kids. That's all." He didn't want to tell her about the condition in which he had found the cows.

"Then you'd better think about driving over there. The day's half done and you know how they hate to bother with us folk here in Woodvine."

"You're right. I just thought that I'd relax a bit before I headed over there." He watched Michelle go out of the kitchen, into the hallway and head for the front door.

"And I've got a lot of cleaning to do for our get-together tomorrow." Her house was immaculately spotless, as usual; she merely needed an excuse to be alone. Davis realized that, and knew well enough not to mention it.

At the front door, he turned to say goodbye.

"Oh, look," she said, pointing. "There goes old Red!" The police cruiser slid by, down the spur toward the forests beyond.

"He gives me the creeps, sometimes. If only we'd known what he was really like," she mused.

"Yeah, maybe then I'd have beaten him those times I ran for mayor."

"Don't you feel too bad about it, Davis. I mean, how could anybody have beaten someone named Red Sage? His name alone was worth half the votes." She laughed.

Laughing with her, Davis patted her cheek, turned and strode down the steps and went to his truck. "I never thought of it that way," he said. "But, by God, I think you're right." Chuckling, he pulled out of the drive and aimed his truck toward Martinsville.

CHAPTER FOUR

Standing before Sheriff Watts, Davis felt older and more of an outsider than he ever had in his entire life. The man was an artist when it came to his particular brand of uncaring arrogance. He just sat there behind his big desk and drew on a soggy, stinking cigar. His cheeks bellowed inward as he sucked on the spit-damp roll of tobacco.

"And just what am I supposed to do about a bear, Mr. Ryan? I ain't no big game hunter. In fact, I ain't never even shot at anything bigger 'n' a rabbit. 'Cept of course for some prisoner or two that took it into their heads to run. Heh heh." He said the last just that way: *Heh heh*, as if a chuckle were something completely alien to him.

Looking over at the pair of smirking young deputies lounging lazily nearby, Davis spoke. "Well, I ain't quite sure it is a bear, sheriff. Mr. Wishon is missing his three hounds in addition to his cows getting killed, so we were thinking that maybe it's some kids or someone doing some vandalism out there."

"But you said this Wishon fella ain't seen anybody around his place." The sheriff leaned forward and began to scribble on a note pad.

"That's right. He hasn't seen anyone, but that doesn't mean they weren't there."

"Besides the two cows and the dogs, was there anything else missin' or vandalized?" He drew the cigar out of his lips, and Davis suddenly wished he hadn't seen him do it.

"Uh, no. He hasn't noticed anything else wrong. But I think that's serious enough, don't you?" Davis shuffled his feet, feeling nervous. He didn't like that; he wasn't accustomed to being made to feel nervous. At least when Ben had been the sheriff he at least made an effort to make you feel like he was interested in your problems. But Ben had been dead for ten years, so that did Davis no good at all.

"I'll tell you what, Mr. Ryan. If I can find the time, tomorrow, I'll send somebody on over to Woodvine and you can take him out to this Wishon fella's place and he'll have a look about."

He leaned back.

"Is that it?"

"What else can I do?"

"Can't you send someone by today?"

"Today?!" The big man was incredulous. "I don't have the time or the manpower to be sending anyone out to this guy's farm just to tell him that I agree that a bear's done killed two of his cows! Who do you think we are? We've got more than enough to keep us busy covering what goes on around here in the real world!"

Davis stared down at the sheriff, at his young, strong forearms revealed from rolled up khaki sleeves. He waited until the sheriff's dark brown eyes met his pale blue ones. "Don't you care about those folk?"

"What folk, old man?"

"Billy and Shelley Wishon. They're both in their eighties, and Shelley's health isn't what it used to be. That's why Billy didn't come to you himself. He doesn't like to leave his wife for too long, and he can't take her roamin' around all over the county every time he gets a mind to."

"Look, Mr. Ryan, I ain't a hardass. I know about old people. Me and my men check up on old folk all around this county—-the ones whose houses get broken into, and the ones who get mugged and robbed. It happens in these parts. So, what you ought to do is feel lucky that the Wishons live so far out in the boonies that no one wants to go that far to mess with them.

"Now, I told you that I would send someone out there to have a look for them, and that's what I'm going to do. But it'll take a day or two to get it done. Okay?"

"I guess if that's all that I can expect of you." Davis turned, and made sure that he did not shuffle out of the air conditioned room.

He felt the eyes of the deputies staring into his back, but he didn't look in their direction. The door clicked shut behind him, and he found himself in the hallway of

Martinsville's county courthouse.

The place bustled with people going about their business. Somewhere in this building there was a file for property tax owed by the residents of the Woodvine community. That idea made his blood boil.

He went home.

CHAPTER FIVE

In the morning, Davis had awakened shortly before sunrise, but not to the familiar crowing of Joe Gunn's prize rooster.

Feeling tired and not completely rested, he got up and fixed his coffee. He still percolated his on top of the stove, and had resisted buying an automatic drip machine. He'd had some coffee from one of the popular contraptions and just plain didn't like it. So he still had his battered percolator that made the good stuff right on top of his gas stove. The smell filled the five-room house and he soon found that he was feeling better from the scent of the coffee. Sitting at the kitchen table, the top all singed from his days as a smoker, he looked up to the wall beside his refrigerator and noticed that today was the fifteenth: time to pay the bills.

Going to his desk, he took a big mug of hot, black coffee with him and he drew out his checkbook and the few bills that he had to pay each month.

First he paid his Georgia Power bill. He smiled, glad that he no longer worked for them, that he had taken his early retirement three months ago. He had enjoyed the job he had last held with the company: that of a meter reader. It had enabled him to get to know the remaining citizens of Woodvine better than he might have.

And he didn't have to travel around the state as an in-house inspector, sizing up all of the substations and nit-shit generators the company had dotted over their territory. Toward the end of that job, all of the driving had really begun to tell on him. But, it was all behind him now. Yes, they gave him his pension once a month, and they got a bit of it back every thirty days, too. He jotted his name on the check and sealed it up, slapped on the stamp.

Next, he drew out the bill from his charge card. He had finally broken down and gotten one of the infernal things, and it was one of the decisions he usually regretted. He had racked up a full 1,000 dollars on it without realizing what he was doing. He had done that much damage in a single month of purchasing new hunting equipment in Macon (and not in Martinsville, thank you) at his favorite sporting goods store. The new rifle, his .220, was a wonderful weapon, but after that orgy of buying, he had put the bit of plastic madness in his sock drawer and there it had remained for almost a year. Signing the one hundred dollar check, he closed it up and kissed it goodbye.

At last, he wrote out his payment for the phone bill--a mere twenty-three dollars--and sat there looking at it. It suddenly occurred to him how few people there in Woodvine still had phones. The local phone company had ceased service to certain land lines when the parties fell below three households. Davis was fairly certain that only those people who lived in the cluster of houses that made up the central part of Woodvine retained their lines. It was an idea that he found especially alarming, driving home the fact of the community's creeping isolation.

When you thought about it, old Billy Wishon hadn't had much choice but to come to him with his problem. Driving to Martinsville would've meant either taking his frail wife on a forty-five minute drive (each way) in the heat of day, or leaving her for two hours or more while he went into town. Davis had really been the man's only option; he was glad that he was there for the farmer.

Rising from his old oak desk, Davis went to his den and parted the curtains on the big window there. He could see his neighbor Joe's back yard where the man kept his chicken coop. This was the first time Davis could recall not having heard the rooster crow at the coming sun. Peering out, he could just discern the big male bird sitting quietly on his favorite perch where he could watch his flock, could pounce on any hen that ventured below him.

The rooster merely sat, moving but slightly, making no effort to announce his position to the world; perhaps he was sick, or just getting too ancient to crow. And that made Davis think again of old Billy and his wife living alone so far from everyone else.

Moving with some speed, he went back to his bedroom. He didn't know why he should worry so, but it seemed to be the thing to do.

In more of a hurry than he was accustomed, Davis pulled on the same clothes he had worn the day before, not bothering with such luxuries as finding something fresh to wear, or even stopping long enough to shave or to brush his teeth. Beard, bad breath, body odor and all, he was going to go out and check on the Wishons. They were depending on him, and damned if he'd leave their welfare up to the whims of an out-of-town cop who couldn't care less for them. Drawing his shoes over his dirty socks, he noticed how his hands were shaking. *What's wrong?* Something was wrong. He could feel it. *Don't be silly. What could be wrong?*

As he lifted his key ring, he heard how it jangled in his shivering fingers. *Shit!* He was scared, and didn't know why.

Outside, the sun coming up over the tops of the pines, he looked into the wall of trees that towered everywhere, surrounding his house, the town, the road out. And he realized how terribly quiet it all was. Nothing stirred. Nothing called out to the new day. Wiping the sleep from his eyes, he rushed then to his truck and started the old girl. He left great swirls of dirty sand billowing in his wake.

The too-fast drive out to the Wishons' farm did nothing to dispel the alarm he felt. All along the way he kept looking to the treetops for birds; he kept his window down to listen for the always-noise of the billions of insects that lived in the undergrowth of the piney woods. Nothing. Not a wing fluttered, not a call was uttered, not once did he hear the wail of some horny bug screaming to couple. He drove through the dying town, thinking of the citizens, his wards, as if they were merely corpses who didn't realize they were dead yet.

Off the spur road, Davis took his half-ton pickup bouncing over the washboard. He did not slow for the rough sections of rippled roadway, and he did not pause to wince as the truck body and undercarriage rang together in quick shrieks. He just pushed the pedal closer to home and let fly.

Up ahead: the post holding the mailbox. He slowed, but not much, and jerked the wheel hard right, took the driveway too fast, he knew, but did it anyway. Thinking of Billy or Shelley suddenly popping from beside the drive, he at last let the pressure off of the gas pedal and applied the brakes. He came to a halt in the front yard of their white frame house. While he waited for the big cloud of dust to settle around him, he watched the front door through the haze of falling sand. Still, nothing moved, nothing made a sound save the idling engine of his aging Chevy, and no one came out of the house.

No one came out of the house.

Slowly, Davis gathered his courage. *No, you idiot. Don't be afraid! There's nothing wrong.* But there was. He'd made enough noise to startle the old couple. He knew that. And he knew that a pair such as they were accustomed to rising much earlier than this, so he knew they were not still sleeping. And if they were awake, why hadn't they come to the front door to greet him? Their truck, their only transportation, was sitting just where it had been when last he'd seen it. The sun, rising over the trees now, speared him in the face. He climbed out of his truck, but he left it running. In case he had to rush back to it.

Moving across the yard, Davis went up the steps to the porch and to the front door. "Hello!" His voice was a ridiculous squeak.

He tried again. "Hello, Billy! Shelley! It's Davis, here! Anybody home?" Better that time. You could almost believe that he wasn't scared out of his mind. At the door, he saw that only the screen was shut. The door itself was opened wide. He rapped on the screen. "Billy! I thought I'd come and check up on you this morning! Shelley?" He sniffed, hunting for the odor of newly fried bacon, of the old woman's famous biscuits baking in the oven. The odors were stale, many hours old. 'No breakfast was cooked here this morning.' At last, he opened the door, the spring groaning rustily. Once more, "Billy?"

To Hell with it. He stepped into the house, going from front to back, room to room. Waiting until the very last, he stepped to the bedroom door, the only one closed tight; it opened with a slight shove. He looked in, saying nothing. The bed was unmade, the covers unkempt, swept aside as if in a great hurry. *Or in a panic.*

Beside the bed, there was a pair of overalls. Davis toed at them, aiming for the pocket and giving it a swift nudge. Keys jangled. *Shit.* He knelt and lifted them, feeling in the worn fabric. Davis drew out the keys to the house, to Billy's truck, to Billy's tractor, to the lock on his loft. Billy wouldn't go off and leave his keys. In fact, he *couldn't* go off and leave his keys. Davis let them drop from his hand.

Afraid, Davis went to the kitchen, and there in the corner was one of Billy's shotguns--the one he'd let Davis carry when they'd gone to the pasture. Billy's own gun was gone. Billy had carried it out with him, obviously. Davis lifted the shotgun that was still there, cracked it to check that it was, indeed, loaded with buckshot, and only then did he venture out into the back yard. The lone sound was the chugging of his truck.

"Billy!" He screamed it. *No, the truck wasn't the only sound.* There was an angry and incessant buzzing coming from the barn. *And where have you heard that before?* In the barn, there was a terrible orchestration of blowflies; they were feeding, laying their fruitful eggs. *In what?*

"Oh, God, Billy. Oh, please, please, no. SHELLEY!" He screamed their names until his throat was raw. He had to go in. He had no choice, because weren't they depending on him? Wasn't he in charge around here? "Please, no." He headed for the barn.

Not pausing to call their names one last time, he crept up to the graying, tractor-sized doorway of the barn. Pulling it open, he was struck in the face by the sheer stench that had occupied the barn like some bloated beast. Out with the stink came a mere cloud or two of swarming flies, their black bodies fat with feasting, tails glittering like obscene rainbows in the bright summer sun. Davis gagged, but he went right on in. He had to see.

There were three stalls to inspect, and he went to them, holding to the splintering, dry wood with one hand, gripping the shotgun in the other, wanting to cover his nose with both, but resisting the urge. He looked into the first: empty. The second held the corpse of Billy's angus bull. Its head had been crushed as if in a gigantic vise. In the third, he found the festering remains of another cow. Huge, gaping wounds puckered inward, outward, entrails flowing from a pierced body cavity. No sign of

Billy. No sign of Shelley. *Thank You, God. Oh, thank You.*

Davis rushed out of the barn, staggering aside as he went into the open sunlight. His wobbling gait took him inadvertently down the side of the building that faced the corn field. He looked that way.

Something had come through the corn. Something very wide had come through the tall corn, shunting it aside as though it were mere blades of yard grass, making an awful pathway through all of that green, green stuff. And there at the end of that path, where yard grass did indeed meet with the corn, Davis found Billy's shotgun lying upon the ground. It appeared to have been bent double as though it were a stick of licorice.

Davis ran then. He did not stop to examine the shotgun. He did not stop to check to see if any of those strange tracks mottled the moist ground of the corn field. He merely rushed to his truck.

And he got the Hell out of there.

CHAPTER SIX

"Get hold of yourself, Davis! Calm down!" Michelle guided him to the big easy chair that had belonged to her husband. She looked at Davis Ryan, self-appointed do-gooder of Woodvine, and what she saw frightened her, for she knew that Davis was a calm and level headed type who would not go to pieces like this without good reason. Patting his back, she waited while he calmed, waited until his breathing became more even.

"Now, one more time; tell me what's wrong."

"It's the Wishons." Davis stared at the rusty pattern of flowers in the worn carpet beneath his dusty shoes. Michelle's husband, Dan, had been about to tear out that old carpet and replace it when he'd suddenly died of heart failure. *Heart failure, yeah. Calm down, boy.* He took a deep breath, held it in.

"And what about the Wishons, Davis? What happened to them?"

Michelle came to the front of the chair, seated herself on the edge of the ottoman there.

"I...I don't know what happened to them." Davis breathed out, felt his heart cease its pounding.

"What do you mean: 'You don't know'?"

"They weren't there. They were gone. Gone." He was feeling better, could feel his self-control returning. *Yeah, the Wishon farm is miles away, now.*

"If they were just gone, then what's the problem? They go into Martinsville to buy their groceries just like everyone else around here. What's the problem?"

"No. They didn't go into Martinsville. Billy's truck was sitting there right where it was the last time I was over there.

It's the only way they have of getting around. You know that." He sat back, sighed, leaned forward again, his head in his hands.

"Davis, would some coffee make you feel better? Something else?"

"Yes. A good cup of black coffee would be fine," he told her.

She got up from where she sat and went to the kitchen. He could hear her back there tinkering with the dishes.

"Don't they have any relatives who come to see them? Maybe someone just dropped in and Billy took that opportunity to drive to town in an air conditioned car. Doesn't that sound logical?"

She yelled that to him from where she was.

"Billy and Shelley haven't seen either of their kids in fifteen years. They don't even know where their daughter lives.

And their son hasn't so much as written to them since God knows when. Besides that, he lives in California. I don't think anyone came out to visit with them."

She was back with his coffee; she handed it to him, and he took a sip of the hot drink. "Well what did you see that spooked you so?"

What could he say? What could he tell her? That he'd really seen nothing? "Billy's angus bull and another one of his cows were in the barn. They were dead, Michelle. Looked like they'd been that way for several hours, at least."

"Do you think someone kidnapped them?"

He thought of that awful trail something had cut through the corn. What could he say about Billy's gun all twisted like it some kind of kid's toy? "I reckon somebody could've kidnapped 'em. But, I don't know. We need to get the sheriff out here. We need to get him out here as soon as we can."

Once more, he felt her hand patting his shoulder, caressing the side of his beard-stubbled face. "You just relax, Davis. I'll go and call the sheriff's department and see if we can't get someone out here." She left him, and he did relax as she went to her phone in the kitchen. He could hear her dial the number—-she still had an old rotary phone--heard her muttering into the phone.

Before she was back, he had actually fallen to sleep. She found the coffee cup sitting in his lap, nearly as full as when she'd brought it to him. Carefully, she picked it up and took it back to the kitchen. Michelle decided to just let him doze.

"What a birthday," she whispered.

By the time he had awakened from the catnap Michelle had allowed him, and by the time he had been able to go to his own house a quarter of a mile from hers to bathe and to change into clean clothes, the sheriff had arrived; the car pulled into his driveway. Davis was waiting for him.

"You wanna take me out to this Wishon place," the officer asked Davis, standing out of his car only grudgingly.

"You really should know how to get out there, Sheriff. Old Ben always knew his way around this county." Davis came down the steps of his porch.

"Ben Hardison's been dead for ten years, old man. I'm the sheriff now, and if you don't like it, then that's just too bad.

Now, do you want to take me out there, or not?"

"Yeah, I'll take you out there." At the passenger side of the car, Davis bent over to peer in through the tinted glass. "Didn't bring any deputy?"

"No, I didn't bring a deputy. Like I told you yesterday, we're busy where I come from, and I don't have the time or the manpower to go chasin' wild geese." With that, Sheriff Watts climbed back into the car. "Get in," he said, reaching over to open the door.

"Now, you tell me what's so important that you can call it an emergency." He began backing out of Ryan's driveway, pulling his reflector shades over his eyes.

"I told you yesterday that something bad was going on over at the Wishon farm, and I was right."

"Are you going to tell me, or are you going to talk my ear off?" The police officer had his car backed into the street and was turning to head out of Woodvine.

"You'll just have to see for yourself when we get out there."

Davis would say no more.

"Then at least tell me how to get there. Shit."

"Just head on out this way until you come to the old Stahl Road." The confused expression on the cop's face was enough for Davis. "That's the third dirt road on the left after we pass the courthouse," he explained. "Old Ben would've..."

"I know, I know. *Ben would've known what you were talking about.* Listen, old man..."

"My name's Ryan. Davis Ryan. I told you that yesterday, too."

Davis did not look at the other man. He kept his eyes front, and glanced aside only when they passed Michelle's house.

"Okay. I'm sorry about that. Look, Mr. Ryan, I'm not trying to be hard about all of this. It's just that I really do have more than my share of work elsewhere."

"I think you better just do what you were elected to do. We can still vote out here in Woodvine, you know. I'm sure somebody out here must have voted for you."

"Shit. Just don't lecture me, okay?" They rode in silence for a while.

"Here," Davis said after a ways. "Turn here." He didn't bother to tell the sheriff about the rough spots, but he did brace himself when they came to them. Sheriff Watts only bumped his head on the ceiling twice. Quickly, they were at the Wishon farm.

"This it?"

"Well, if we went any further, we'd be drivin' through trees. Just turn down the driveway here." They did.

Getting out of the car, the two stood and looked around.

Everything was just as Davis had left it. The officer reached into the auto from where he stood and he tooted the horn a couple of times. No one came out to greet them.

"Are you sure nobody visited here and gave them a ride somewhere?" Sweat was beading on Watts' face. He was unaccustomed to being without his air-conditioned spaces.

"Yes, we're sure. And we called the County General to make sure that they didn't send any ambulance out here. There ain't nobody named Wishon checked into the hospital there or been admitted to the emergency room."

"Well, they must be somewhere." They went toward the house.

Going through the rooms, Davis noticed that nothing was changed from his brief visit. Except...

"I don't see his keys," Davis said.

"What?"

"His keys. I left his keys layin' on top of his overalls where I dropped them." The clothing was there in a crumpled heap. He nudged at them. No keys. "His wallet's still here, but the keys are gone."

"Any money in it?"

Davis looked. "Yeah. A hundred or more." No one had robbed them, at least. "But where's the keys?"

"Let's go take a look in the barn. His cattle are dead, you say?" The two clumped out of the room, their steps sounding loud and hollow in the empty home.

"Yeah," Davis told him as they came to the back yard. "His bull and another cow are dead in the barn there." He stopped and looked, the barn doors standing much wider than when he'd left.

"What's wrong?"

"I didn't leave those doors standing that far open." He went up to the barn, the sound of feeding blowflies no less loud than before. They went in.

"See? Both of 'em. Something completely crushed the bull's head right in." The sheriff had seen enough, and moved quickly out of the stinking building. Following him, Davis saw that the tractor was gone from its place in the barn.

"Where are you going, Ryan," Watts asked as the older man went around the side of the barn. He followed.

"Damn!"

"What is it?"

Davis looked into the corn field. On the far side, at the end of that space something huge had made in the corn rows, was Bill Wishon's tractor. Someone had driven it out there, covering what tracks they may have found in the earth, making it seem as if the tractor had been what had mashed its way through the corn stalks. It certainly looked as if that's what had done the damage to the field. He went to the spot where the bent gun had lain. The gun, of course, was gone.

"Billy's gun is gone. And the tractor wasn't over there when I was out here this morning." He pointed at the machine at the opposite side of the field.

"Are you sure it wasn't there?"

"Positive, Sheriff. I may be gettin' old, but I'm not senile!"

"I wasn't sayin' you were, Mr. Ryan. I was just askin' if you were sure, that's all."

"I'm more than sure. I'm positive. The tractor was in the barn, and the gun was lyin' right here!" He indicated a space on the grass. Indeed, he could see where something hairpin shaped had been pressed into the ground. "See that," Davis asked. "You can see right where it was layin'."

"Yeah. Somethin' was there." Watts pulled a kerchief from his shirt pocket and dabbed at his face, then he began walking through the route that had been cut through the corn. Davis remained where he was, watching until the sheriff got to the tractor, climbed upon it for a moment, then hopped down. Holding his hand up, he called to Davis. "Here's the keys!" He hustled back.

"Now, show me those other dead cows, why don't you?"

"Okay." They went around the corn field to the pasture, went over the fence and to the rotted corpses.

There were less of the bodies than when Davis had last seen the dead animals--the maggots and such had done one hell of a job on the rotting flesh. What remained of the animals seemed to be merely drying cowhide draped over a scaffolding of bones. The stench was still powerful, though.

"Where are you going, Mr. Ryan?"

"I'm just going to look over here in this bare spot." He didn't say that there had been some kind of huge bird track in the sand the day before. Again, the thing he'd been looking for was gone. It almost looked as if someone had scraped over the spot with a broom or...

"What are you doing, now?" Watts looked on as Davis went to the fence and reached through it. The old man stood holding a pine branch in his hand. "What are you doing with that," he asked.

"It's a branch. That's all. Just a branch." He held the green bit of vegetation to his nose and sniffed the spot where it had been broken from the tree. It still smelled fresh, the needles were still green. Searching, he even saw the tree from which it had been wrenched; a thumbnail sized ball of resin had formed where the branch had come free: very fresh--less than an hour old.

Someone had used it to wipe out the strange track he and Wishon had seen, and their own track, also.

"God, it's hot! Let's get out of here." Turning, the officer headed back toward the farmhouse.

His eyes searching the line of trees that bordered the pasture and the fields, Davis finally tossed the branch down and followed the sheriff. He didn't want the other man to be out of his sight, for Davis had not brought a gun with him. A gun was something he wasn't going to go without for a while. Until someone had this mess cleared up to Ryan's satisfaction.

Once they had returned to the Wishon's home, the two went to the officer's car and got in.

"What are you going to do, sheriff?" Davis now dabbed at his own face with the corner of a kerchief he had brought.

"Well, there ain't too much I can do. I have to wait for a while before I can declare them officially missin'. After that, we can put out a bulletin with other law enforcement agencies, and maybe we can get out here with a search party. Civil Defense guys can help out on that, maybe the forest service can come in on it, too."

"What?! Why can't you get somebody out here to look for 'em now?" Davis stared incredulously at the big sheriff.

"I told you. I have to wait a while before we can take any action that's goin' to use up a lot of man hours."

"Man-hours?! We're talkin' about two people here! Man hours?! You can do better than that!"

Watts did his best to hold in his anger. As the sheriff of

Marten County, he was not accustomed to anyone questioning his authority, or to anyone raising their voice to him. Still, he would do his best to humor the old man. "Look," he paused. "If you're really humpin' to get those folk found--and nobody but you has even said they're lost--then I will authorize you to gather up a search party and go lookin' for them your own self. How does that sound?"

"It ain't a matter of you bein' able to authorize me to do it. It's a matter of whether or not you can stop me." Davis set his jaw and glared at the young sheriff, or at the reflection of himself that glared back from the reflector shades the other man had pulled over his eyes.

"Well, now," Watts said, holding it in, "you do that, why don't you? Just get some of your buddies up and go lookin' for the Wishons. And if you find them, then please feel free to give me a call." He started the car and pulled away from the deserted

Farm house.

The two sat in silence thereafter.

CHAPTER SEVEN

If nothing else, Red Sage still felt a sense of responsibility for Woodvine. While it was true that he would never admit, even to himself, that the town's decline was due almost exclusively to his back room political dealings, he had to confess that not all of his decisions regarding the welfare of Woodvine had been well thought out. At any rate, he yet kept his ear to the ground and was ready to pick up on any event that might mean at least a temporary respite in the downward slide for his fellow citizens. It was so with this latest development.

"Red, what in the world is going on around here? What are you up to?" Raymond Weller sat in the front seat of the police cruiser, sweating in the vehicle. As the once-pastor of the defunct Woodvine Baptist Church, he had quite a lot of patience, especially for his old friends who were growing old along with him. But he didn't much care for being taken from the comfort of his home to satisfy the whims of a man who was obviously not terribly far from senile. "And do we have to go riding about in this old cruiser? For Heaven's sake, Red! It isn't even air conditioned! Where is your Cadillac?"

"Ray, I don't mind suffering a little when it comes to the welfare of my fellow citizens. How do you feel about sacrificing some comfort to help out someone else? It seems I've heard you give a sermon or two on that very subject. Now, don't you think that you can sweat some to help out a bit?" Ever the politician, he knew how to twist the knife, and precisely where to stick it, too.

"Of course I'm willing to suffer some to help out a friend in need, but I would also like to know just what is going on." It was times like this that he had his doubts about how dull Red's senses had become. The ex-mayor could still be the fast talking, gabby politician he had been since his youth. "Now, if you don't mind..."

"Of course, Reverend." Red called Raymond *Reverend* whenever he wanted something from the minister. "We've got a problem out at Billy Wishon's farm. And I thought that if you were with me, I could talk some fellows into helping out with it."

Slowly, the two drove down Woodvine's old Main Street, the preacher wishing Red would drive faster so that he could at least get a decent breeze blowing through the window. "What's wrong out at the Wishons' farm. Is it Shelley Wishon? I've heard that she isn't getting along too well these days. Did she pass on?" He didn't have his congregation any longer, the church was a moldering building just off the spur outside of town, but he still did his best to keep up on former members, and to see them from time to time, if he could.

"Well, yes, but it isn't just Shelley. It's the two of 'em, I think." They went past Davis Ryan's house, and both were quiet.

The Reverend knew how Red still considered Davis something of a rival for the town's attention and affection. Although Raymond had to admit that there wasn't much affection left for the former mayor.

"They didn't both pass away, did they? Why hasn't someone called me about this?" He fumed, not accustomed to hearing news of this kind second hand. Usually, Widow Jarman called him with news of the latest death in the community. The woman had edited the church bulletin back in the days when the church had still existed, and she'd always been something of a ghoul, at any rate.

"Well, I didn't say they were dead, Reverend." Davis Ryan's house was behind them.

"Then what's the problem? Are they both ill? What?" He was growing a bit less patient; he dabbed at his face with a handkerchief pulled from his left back pocket: RM was embroidered in one corner--he paused to look, recalling the girl who'd made the kerchiefs for him so long ago.

"No, they aren't ill, either."

"Then what?!" He actually raised his voice, feeling the heat and the sweat beginning to trickle down his lean neck.

"They're missing. They're both missing." Red slowed the police car even further and angled the vehicle toward a driveway.

"Missing? Are you sure? Maybe they just went in to Martinsville for a while. Has anyone checked with the hospital there?

"What? Are we stopping to see Kiser? Why are you going to Kiser's house, Red? You know I can't abide that man!" Raymond Weller was pulling at his collar, now, feeling the heat at its worst, and feeling something else, also. His throat was swelling, it seemed.

"Yes, we're going to see Mark! If we're going to organize a search party, then I think he's the best man for the job." Stopped in the sandy drive of the two-story Victorian home, Red turned in his seat and stared over at his rider.

"Now, I am going to try to do something for this town. It's important that I do this. It..." He paused, staring away, perhaps into the past. "It's something that I need to do for Woodvine," he said, finding the words. "We've all of us been dying here, just rotting away. We need something like this to pull us out of the nosedive we've been in for too long. I know you don't care for Mark, but I need both of you if we're going to do this right. Okay?"

Weller wiped at his reddened face with the now damp kerchief. "Alright," he gave in. "Just tell me what it is that you want us to do."

Getting out, Red waited as the revered opened his own door and climbed from the oven of a car. "Why, we're going to organize us a search party, Raymond. And *we're* going to lead it." He didn't have to say: *And not Davis Ryan.*

The front door of the Victorian opened, and Mark Kiser stepped out. He was as ugly and as brutish as Reverend Weller remembered him, all those years sitting in the middle pew of the church, every Sunday, never missing a service, no matter what. The man had been as great a hypocrite as any he had known, and as evil, too. Swallowing, the preacher followed Red up to the house,

Kiser staring hard at him all the way, an awful laugh in those sunken, cruel eyes. Kiser didn't have to laugh at the minister; not out loud, at least.

At the door, the three men converged, handshakes were exchanged. Not all of the mayor's old cronies were dead.

"What's going on over there?" Sheriff Watts said, not exactly asking his passenger. He slowed the car so that he could get a better look.

Davis leaned forward, peering through the tinted glass at the people gathered in front of Mark Kiser's house. There were twenty or more people there, all of them listening to someone speaking to them from the top step of Kiser's front porch. "That's Red Sage," Davis said.

"Red Sage? Red Sage..." Watts let the name roll about in his mind, trying to place it, too young to recall the man right away.

"He used to be mayor when Woodvine used to be a town," Davis reminded him.

"Oh, yeah! Ain't he the old coot who rides around in that '57 Chevy? The one with Woodvine Police on it?" Watts was ready to make a remark about it, but remembered where he was, and who was with him.

"'58."

"What?"

"It's a '58 Chevy. Not a '57. Wouldn't you know it?" Ryan eyed the group of people, all of whom he recognized. "Stop here, how 'bout it?"

"Sure, sure. I wanna hear him, anyway. What he's sayin'."

He pulled over on the left shoulder, touching Kiser's yard with his new Ford, and the two got out to listen.

Red's voice was loud, and to hear him, you wouldn't have thought that he was eighty years old.

"We're not trying to alarm anyone, and we don't know that Bill and Shelley Wishon aren't perfectly alright somewhere. But I think that if we're to do the Christian thing, then we need to organize a search party and go out there and see if we can't do something to help them.

"Of course Reverend Weller here was as upset about it as I was, and he's behind me one hundred per cent. And Mark Kiser was kind enough to lend me his front step here, and has also volunteered to lead a party. Now, what we're going to need is about ten able bodied men to go along with us to the Wishon farm so that we can make a thorough search of the vicinity." Red ignored the sheriff's department cruiser he'd seen park within his line of sight. He was on a roll, and this was his town.

"And we'll need the ladies to keep us supplied with good food and cool drinks when we come back in from tromping through the woods. I know that I can count on you good people."

Some of the folk had turned their backs on him to see who had driven up. He raised his voice even louder to regain their attention.

"A lot of people think Woodvine's a dead town, a ghost town, a foregone conclusion that we're done for. But I know better! I know we're not a ghost town." To hear him, you could almost believe that the boarded up storefronts were still bustling with business, that the rotting church was still the spiritual center of a thriving community, that the closed and moldering schools were yet daytime home to hundreds of squealing children, that there were even children still abiding in the almost dead place known as Woodvine. People listened to him.

"We've still got a lot of citizens here who love this city. And I don't think those people would fall down and give up when someone needs them!

"Now, do I have anyone willing to volunteer?"

There was a collective call as most of the thirty or so people who had gathered from the neighborhood yelled back to him. "Yes," they told him. "I'll help." Then, "What do you want us to do?" someone asked.

"Ha ha!" Watts took his shades off as he bellowed at the former mayor of Woodvine. "You should o' run for county commissioner last time out! I think you would o' won!"

Red's face took on a stunned, blank expression, as if someone had suddenly struck him, as if someone had informed him that the electric lamp he'd been using as a paperweight could be plugged in and used to illuminate a dark room. He recovered quickly, though, trying not to think of lost opportunities, of mistakes made too long ago to rectify. Standing, he watched the chuckling sheriff climb back into his car and start it up.

"You people let me know what you turn up," the officer called as he pulled away. "You have my blessings." He drove off, leaving Davis Ryan on the fringes of the crowd standing at Sage's feet.

Sage had to hold back a smile in spite of anything else.

CHAPTER EIGHT

The half mile back to his house was longer, hotter than Davis had remembered. He felt the thick, wet breaths billowing in and out of his chest, felt the steamy air pressing about him beneath the afternoon sun. His legs were growing tired as he trudged along in the loose, sandy soil of the shoulder. He would have walked on the surer footing of the road, but the asphalt was so hot, glowing like wet tar, that he could feel the sun radiating up through the cuffs of his pants as he moved atop it.

The sweat ran down his legs. He could feel his socks growing damp with each step. His shirt clung to his back, to his arms. His hair was plastered to his skull, and he was wishing that he hadn't been too stubborn to ask that Watts drive him back to his house. God, he hated getting old.

Here he was, walking along a road he had walked along too many times to recall, and the journey had never been so bad, so difficult, so tiring. He remembered once carrying a sixty-pound sack of seed from beyond the courthouse all the way to Wesley Jarman's place a mile farther from where he now stood. And that had also been in the heat of midday, in the hottest part of August. But he'd been so young, then. *So damned young.*

Davis wanted a drink. Anything would have done, as long as it was cold. He wanted to sit in his easy chair in the front room with the air conditioner on and not even a book to read. He just wanted to kick back with something cold, maybe a beer, maybe some lemonade, maybe just some water with ice cubes rattling around in the glass, clinking there in his hand, the dew getting his fingers wet. That's what he wanted, because he was hot, he was tired, he was getting old.

Sixty-one, Davis Ryan. He stopped, looking down the road.

Skeeter Archer lived in the brick ranch-style house with the blue trimmed shutters just to his left across the street. Skeeter had known him since the man had moved to Woodvine back in '69 when he'd come to rebuild the new sawmills Stahl's Lumber Yard had brought in, back when the town had been thriving and vital.

Old Skeeter had met Nina Vincent, (the niece of Monroe Vincent who had been the town pharmacist), had ended up marrying Nina, and the two had built that very house. Nina was gone (cancer), and certainly Skeeter, (his real name was Simon), enjoyed rare company, so now would be as good a time as any to drop in and see the man. Why, the first thing he'd do would be to offer a drink to Davis.

Yeah, you're sixty-one years old and that's too old to be walking down this road in the hottest part of day in the hottest month of the year. There's no shame in taking a break. Or two.

Davis knew more people along the way. *Sixty-one, old man.* He stopped, his hands on his hips, and he looked down the narrow road, at the water oaks in yards, at the few houses that stood between here and his own which he could just make out past the bend there. *Old man. Sixty-one-year-old, old man.*

No, he thought. *I can do it without stopping to beg for water.* He went on.

On his left was Mary Scott's house, sitting small and green with its little lawn that was probably too brown, but there hadn't been a lot of rain lately. She was too frail to be out in the sunlight watering that lawn, and John, her husband, had been dead for several years, so he wasn't around to do it. How old had John been, anyway? The man hadn't graduated from Woodvine High too many years before Davis had. Sixty-three. Yes, he remembered now; because John had died at sixty-three, just the same as Davis' father had.

Heredity, old man. Daddy dead at sixty-three, Momma at sixty-five. Doesn't sound too good for you, now does it? Split the difference and what does that leave? Sixty-four, Davis. How does sixty-four sound? Or maybe sixty-one. Dead at sixty-one of a heat stroke in the middle of what used to be Main Street at the tail end of the existence of what had once been the town of Woodvine, Georgia. Think someone will put that on your tombstone, old man? Who'll be left to do that for you?

And then he looked up and there was Michelle's house, an oasis shimmering in the sun, looking almost like a mirage.

When she opened the door, she was going to say *Davis, what did you find at the Wishon farm?* Instead she said nothing. She took one look at the sweating, disheveled figure standing at her threshold and knew enough to take him by the hand and lead him indoors where it was cool. She sat him down in her husband's old easy chair, noting how well Davis settled into it, and she patted his face dry with the hand towel tucked into the big front pocket of her apron.

"Lord, Davis! You look about fit to pass...out," she uttered, holding back the word she had almost said. Michelle felt a shiver, recalling how her husband had looked the day he had died, coming in from painting the back of the house. His face had been bright red, and she had realized after one glance at his expression that something was terribly wrong. Then his skin had gone pale, then gray, and he had barely had time to reach their bed before he had collapsed. She had always been glad of that, at least; that he had died at home, in their bed, and that they had been together.

Davis looked almost as her husband had that last moment before his heart had failed him. Michelle cupped Davis' too hot face in her cool, soft hands. "Don't you know better than to exert yourself in weather like this? Don't you?!" There was more than a little anger in her voice.

"I just didn't think a short walk would do this to me. That's all. I never realized." His eyes had a sad, faraway look. A tear appeared in the corner of his eyelid, then crept slowly down his cheek, joining the salty beads of sweat there. Michelle wiped it away with her towel and did not mention it.

"I'm going to get you a big glass of cold water, Davis. Are you going to be okay while I run back to the kitchen?" She thought of how quickly her husband had faded. He couldn't have waited while she went even so short a distance for anything.

"Yes, Michelle. I'll be okay. And a glass of water sounds very good." He watched her turn and move into the hallway, waiting until she was in the kitchen before he let out the long sigh that was almost a sob. He held it in, though, and did not break down and cry as he felt he certainly must. *Old, old, ineffectual man.*

She called from the back. "Why didn't that sheriff bring you back to your house?"

"Oh, he dropped me off in front of Mark Kiser's place where Red Sage was standing out in front with Reverend Weller. Had a bunch of the neighbors listening to him gab on about getting up a search party for the Wishons." Christ, Davis didn't want to be part of anything that bastard organized.

"Then they really are missing?" Her voice was louder as she came back toward the den. She was there, offering the tall, clear glass of ice water.

"Yes." He wanted to say that they were dead, but he didn't want to upset Michelle. "But how in Hell did Red find out about it so soon? I haven't told anyone but you."

Michelle thought for a moment. "I didn't say anything to anyone else about it. But you know I'm on a party line, Davis. Lois Jarman is on it, and so is Mary Scott. And you know what a gossip Lois is. You'd still think she's doing the church newsletter. She always was a nosy-body."

"A nosy-body, yes." Davis found a smile. Michelle was the only person he'd ever heard use that term, but he liked it. The description seemed terribly appropriate for the Jarman widow. "She probably was listening in, and I'll bet she was right on the phone to the Reverend as soon as you hung up from calling the sheriff. I always did think she was trying to get into his pants, anyway."

"Davis! Now who's acting like a nosy-body?"

He laughed at her, and he could see that she was relieved to see him smiling, could see the genuine concern in her face that he had been too ill to see when she'd opened the door to him. *Ask her to marry you, you idiot! Do it now!*

"Michelle..."

"Hm?"

"Why don't we..." He paused, thinking.

"Why don't we *what*?"

Aw, you're just an old bachelor. Forget it! "Why don't we get my party rolling a little early?" He stared into his half empty glass, and not at her. Had she realized what he had almost asked her? He hoped not.

"What for? I've got a lot of sandwiches to make up before the guests get here. But I reckon we could." She sat before Davis, on the ottoman at his feet.

"I want to talk with Pat, maybe with a couple of the other fellows. I want to take a look around the Wishon place, but I don't want to go with that bunch that Sage is getting up." *And I don't want to go back there by myself,* he thought and did not say.

"Look here, Davis. You almost passed out on my doorstep from walking about in this darned heat for less than half a mile, and I don't want to see you out in the woods stumbling around in the bushes while ticks crawl down your shirt and snakes bite at your feet and the sun burns your fool head off. Don't you have a lick of sense?"

"I'll be careful. We'll take along some coolers and we'll be together and I'll be careful," he told her. "But I want to take a look without that Sage and Kiser hanging around. I don't trust those two."

"And what can you do over there that they can't? They're going to traipse through just as much brush as you can, and there'll probably be more of them, too.

"And just what will you be taking in those coolers, anyway?" she added.

Again, Davis smiled at her. Maybe being married wouldn't be so bad. He liked the idea of someone worrying over him. *Ask her.*

"Just some co' colas, Michelle. Maybe a beer or two."

"A beer or two. I'll bet."

"You care if I give Pat Wilson a call, now? Get him over here as soon as I can?"

"No, Davis, I don't care."
He drained the glass and handed it to her.

CHAPTER NINE

In the end, the gathering was a small one, as Davis had hoped it would be. That was another thing about Michelle that he liked: she seemed to be able to read him, there really was no reason that they would not be able to live together, he reckoned. If only he could stand the change, if only he could just stop being a stubborn old bachelor, like his friend, Pat.

When, at last, the sandwiches had been eaten, and the *Happy Birthdays* had been sung, Davis let Michelle keep the dozen or so others entertained as he steered Pat Wilson toward the back yard where they could talk. They moved slowly about the yard there, taking in the garden that Michelle's husband had laid out years ago, at the garage he had built years ago, at the little rocked in walkways he had dug years ago. At last, they sat down on a wide, whitewashed bench that Dan had also built sometime not too many years back.

"What's bothering you, Davis? I mean, besides just you gettin' old. I can tell when somethin's eatin' at you." And that was true enough. Davis and Pat Wilson had been friends since they'd been school children. Even their fathers had been friends working together in the slash pine forests as cutters back in the days when all the work had been done with great handsaws and long wagons pulled by mules and all of the rest of the labor handled by the black men who had once lived in Woodvine in numbers as great as the whites.

"I don't know how much you've heard about what's been going on at the Wishon place down the old Stahl Road." He looked questioningly at the shorter, stockier man, relieved, in a way, to see that Pat was aging every bit as much as he was. At least he didn't have to feel so alone about it.

"Some, Davis. I picked up a bit from Wesley Jarman on the way over. And I have to tell you that Mark Kiser called me to ask if I would help with a search party to look for the Wishons tomorrow." He scratched at his closely cut scalp, rubbing his nails through red hair gone mainly to white.

"What'd you tell him?"

"I told him that I'd help out if I could. What did you expect me to tell him? Hell, Dave, I don't know those people like you do, but I can't say no to helpin' out an old couple just because you don't get along with Kiser and Sage. You cain't get mad about that, can you?" He batted at a mosquito buzzing about his ear, missed the damned thing.

"No, of course not." Davis leaned forward, his hands covering his mouth. He thought.

"Are you gonna help out with it?"

"They ain't asked me, Pat. And if they did, I don't know if I could stand bein' that close to those two. And maybe takin' orders from 'em, or at least them actin' like they could order me around. I know the both of 'em would get a real kick out of that!"

"Listen. Why don't you go with me? Me an' you could cut out on our own, take in a section without them around, and nobody could tell you how to do what you think needs to be done. How 'bout it?"

"Sure, Pat. That sounds good." He leaned back in the bench, looking at the sun that was beginning to ease behind the pines.

The sky was a pale orange going to purple in the east. Stars were starting to appear in the darkening overhead. "Did they say anything about bringing firearms?"

"Firearms!? Hell, no! Why in the Hell would I need to bring a gun?" He slapped again at the mosquito, his hand smacking against the side of his own face. "Got you, you bastard!" There was a small smear of red where the insect had died on his unshaved cheek. He looked at his hand, wiped the blood away.

"Take your deer rifle, Pat. Your 30.06, if it's cleaned and ready." He said it: *thirty ought six*.

"My deer rifle? What for, Dave? All we're doin' is huntin' for some old folk who maybe wandered off, right?"

"Pat, if I thought that they had only wandered off, then I'd be out there lookin' for 'em right this second. I would. Billy came to me for help, and I didn't do too good a job of it, did I?

"But I don't think they're out in those woods just lost.

Hell! Billy lived out at that farm all of his life. He was born out there. And, maybe, if his Shelly did wander off and got lost, and if he went in to find her, then he would've come back with her. But I don't think that's what happened, at all." He stared into the shadows creeping out, it seemed, from the trees all around the community. The usual orchestra of insects was silent this night (a lone mosquito notwithstanding); he noticed that as it became ever darker.

"Then what do you think did happen to them?" Pat held his breath, waiting to hear the answer. Inside, some ladies were laughing at something someone had said, and sixty-two year old Pat Wilson--lifelong bachelor, a failure at romance--realized that the laugh of old women was much different from that of young girls--he pondered this admittedly silly thought as he breathlessly awaited his best friend's terrible answer. Warm, yellow light spilled into the back yard from the rectangle of the kitchen door as someone opened it, spat, and shut it.

"I ain't sure, Pat." He couldn't look at his lifelong pal.

"Well, if you ain't sure, then tell me what you think."

"I...I don't know *what* I think." He really couldn't put it into words.

"Dave, that sounds stupid! It really does!" Wilson stood up, paced away a few feet and turned to look at Davis.

"I know it doesn't make sense, Pat. But listen. Somethin' killed Billy's cattle. I saw 'em. They were torn up into pieces!

Legs off, guts out, blood everywhere! And when I went back there later, his bull had its head caved right in! Now, what does that?

"Huh?" Davis did not want to be at odds with his best friend. He wanted the other man to understand how he felt, but he didn't know how without sounding crazy.

"Well, somebody just bashed it over the head with a sledge, Dave. Somebody cut up his cows."

"No. Huh-uh. That bull's head was smashed up like it was pressed in a vise or somethin'."

"Somebody hit it more than once. Or maybe a bear did it. Kiser mentioned something about a bear."

"I hope it is a bear, Pat. Because if it's a bear, then I don't think I have to worry about Bill and Shelly. If it's a bear, then I don't think it would come around there lookin' to hurt that poor old couple out by themselves with no one to help them. God, Pat! They came to me for help!"

Davis was standing then, his hands opened stiffly, his arms jutting out by his sides. "They asked me for some help, and what good did I do 'em?"

"Davis! Calm down." Pat's strong hand was on his shoulders, and he did feel some of the tension going out of him at the touch. Davis reached up, rubbing at his temples.

"Those people were counting on me, Pat."

"There ain't nothin' you can do, Dave. Nothin' except go out and look for them tomorrow when it's light out and we can see what we're doin'. What else could you have done that you didn't do?"

"I don't know, Pat. I don't know." He looked away from his friend, from the house, once more gazing into the dark woods that closed them in.

"Let's go back in, for now, Dave. We can get together in the morning and we'll go on out Stahl Road with the rest of 'em and see what we can see. Okay?" Pat slapped his pal on the back, trying to steer him to the house.

"Okay, Pat." They headed back, silent, treading rock-lined paths laid out by a dead man.

"Kind of quiet tonight, ain't it?" This, as they got to the back step.

"What?"

"Quiet. It's kind of quiet out here. The woods are usually kind of noisy when the sun goes down. But not tonight."

Davis looked back at the black, uninviting wall of trees that were just beyond Michelle's neat little yard. "Yeah, you're right. It's too damned quiet out there." He pulled the door shut behind them as they went in to join the others.

CHAPTER TEN

Davis blinked.

He was awake, feeling very rested after the party, after his stomach had filled with sandwiches and cold beer, after Pat had left and the other guests had wandered off, disappearing into the night beyond the spill of the yellow light that stood guard at Michelle's front door.

Davis had watched them all fading into the thick shadows that were only so dark in southern locales, as if the black dust that mixed with the powdery sand were somehow part of the shadows of a muggy August night.

For a moment, Davis lay there in his own bed, thinking of the time he had spent lingering at Michelle's, talking with her, staying long after the others had gone and were only muttered whispers moving down the road.

The lazy minutes he had shared with Michelle had been pleasant, sitting together on her sofa as the blue light from her television played over the two of them where they sat and spoke, not really listening to the sounds yattering at them, not really watching the pictures moving across the screen in front of them.

In a while, the talk had faded, as the guests had faded, and they had merely sat, side by side, staring first at the inane offerings of the television, then at the empty space between themselves and the screen, then (at last) into one another's eyes.

No, they had not made passionate love there on the fading, sturdy sofa. It wasn't that neither of them felt the need or the urge, it just hadn't seemed the thing to do. While lust may not have been merely an old memory lost in the decades since their youths, there was merely a restraint in the both of them that held them back, just a bit.

And so, they had merely touched, their hands meeting coyly, finger finding finger, twining absently, oblivious of arm and shoulder and more.

And so, Michelle had merely placed her head against Davis' chest, she feeling the thickness of his torso, he realizing how small she was, how soft her hair that he could smell clean against his cheek as he lowered his chin to touch.

And so, Davis had placed his hand beneath her chin, lifting her face so that their eyes could meet at last with no others prying at them, invading their intimacy. His were brown like caramels that once were sold in big, clear jars that sat atop glassy showcases in general stores that were now old memories.

Hers were green like the water he had seen in a lake in Mexico when he had been thirty years old and on the road--even then the lake had excited a memory of her, the mistake he could not take back. Their sighs had been all the discussion they had needed.

And so, they had kissed, cuddling for long minutes, drowning, for a time, in sweet nostalgia and present company.

The walk home had been short, and Davis had hardly remembered that the night was unnaturally quiet, had hardly recalled that things did not seem right with all that he knew. He'd hardly had the presence of mind to be a little frightened as he made his way through the moonless dark to his own unlit house where he had undressed and gone quickly to bed and to sleep.

He blinked again, but not to dislodge the sand from his eyes.

He was wide awake, as he was whenever he rose in the mornings just before the sun popped above the horizon and Joe Gunn's rooster crowed to the world. Blinking, he was aware that the sun was not painting the sky that pale lavender of predawn illumination, and Mr. Gunn's bird was not calling out its name. In fact, it was damned dark, the dark of night in the depths of night. Sitting up, he decided that it couldn't have been too many minutes since he had come back to his bedroom. He must have merely dozed for a moment or two.

Then he realized that the light in his kitchen was on, when he knew damned well that he had turned it off before he had gone to his bedroom. Quietly, he went to his dresser and opened his sock drawer and hefted the chrome weight of his .357 revolver. It felt good in his hand, clean and well oiled. And loaded. With great care he crept out of his bedroom, pushing the door open (and glad that he oiled the hinges as well as he oiled his guns) and sneaking barefoot into the hallway.

Looking down the length of the hall, he could see shadows moving in the kitchen: a pair of them, it seemed. *It could be Pat,* he mused, but he could not imagine why his friend would come unannounced into his home in the black of night. Pat knew he kept a loaded pistol near his bed, and Michelle knew it, too. *Who could it be?*

He thought of the Wishons, knowing that whoever had harassed them, had (maybe) kidnapped them, might also think that the entire over aged community of Woodvine was easy pickings for some young thugs heady with youthful power. Well, then, he and the .357 had some new information for them.

Moving carefully, he went to the kitchen, his gun partially raised in front of him, his cotton pajamas making no sound as he went so slow atop the thin carpet. Gun ready, he stepped into the kitchen.

His jaw dropped open, the gun going down to his side at the end of his now limp right arm. He didn't quite drop it, though.

Billy and Shelly Wishon were sitting at the small table in his kitchen. They looked up at him as he entered, their faces expressionless, both of them looking precisely as they had when he had left them days ago.

"Billy! Shelly!" He let out a sigh.

They looked at him, but did not speak. God, the night was quiet.

"Are y'all okay?" he was finally able to ask. He leaned against the doorjamb, all but ready to collapse from the shock of it all. *They're here,* he thought. *They're here!*

"We're mad at you, Davis."

He almost did not hear Billy say that, only barely registering the statement. "Where the hell have you been?" It was all he could think to ask them at the moment.

"Why, we've been dead, Davis," Billy said to him.

And then Davis could hear that the night was not quite so silent as he had thought. There was a muted, but tremendous buzzing coming from somewhere. He'd heard that sound several times in recent days.

"Why, we've just been fucking dead," Billy reiterated, this time blowflies exploding from the black hole of his mouth, flying out in a huge cloud that rose to the ceiling and down and out and all about. "We've just been dead!" The corpse of Billy screamed and that of Shelly stood, her belly heavy with something, Davis could see. And as she stood, that heavy weight inside her succeeded in tearing free, spilling the baggage of turgid entrails and feasting, soupy maggots that flowed out toward Davis' bare feet as he stood frozen in place.

"We've just been dead!" They sang it together, an orchestration of flies.

Screaming, Davis sat up in his lonely bed, staring wide-eyed into his bedroom, seeing that the sun had risen in the sky, that he had slept right through Mr. Gunn's rooster's crowing, that it was morning and not night and that he was not standing in his kitchen watching Billy and Shelly Wishon disintegrate before his staring eyes.

Alone, he sat and clutched his knees and waited until the tears stopped flowing.

They asked me for help. They asked me for help. They asked me...

CHAPTER ELEVEN

Far away, beyond the farthest farm, past the final sandy road that led down to the outermost residence that could remotely be called a part of Woodvine, Addie Lacher lived. You could drive a car to within a mile of her house if you didn't mind scratching the paint job on iron like brambles and jutting palmetto fronds. If you had a good, tough truck, you could pull it to within fifty yards of her tin roofed cabin which sat beneath huge, longleaf pines that were almost as old as Addie. And at ninety-three she was easily the oldest living thing around Woodvine.

She stayed all alone there in her piney grove, had lived that way since her last man had died back before they'd sent William, her only son, to die fighting that Hitler fellow. She'd told him not to go; but he hadn't listened to her, and now he was dead. If he'd done as she'd told him, he would've lit off for the nearest railway yard and hit the road. Not long after that, her man, Roy, had died of the heat. And maybe a little more of grief than of the heat as he'd cut those pulp logs for the Stahl family. Roy hadn't been William's father, but the way the man had carried on, you would have thought so. Grief. What good was it?

She had been prepared for all of that, way back when. She had dreamt of it, and she had had visions. Addie Lacher had a gift for that kind of thing. Always had, even when she was just a girl.

She'd seen a red cloud cover the sun when she was six years old, and the next day her daddy had gotten himself killed in downtown Woodvine--run down by a wagon loaded with four by fours. Once, she had awakened late at night dreaming of white snakes burrowing through her bed, twining about her legs. And then she had known why her sister, Aline, had been so quiet for weeks--and she had not been surprised when Aline had given birth to that high yellow chap seven months later. It was just that way with her.

The season her boy had died she had dreamed of waving to him from a high hilltop, waving to him and to Roy, the both of them standing in a green little valley down below her until a snowstorm came up and the white stuff had hidden them from her.

Addie had never seen snow, but she knew that was what it was when it had paled over her two men. The dream had awakened her, and she had reached over to hold Roy and pull him close. *You sure are cold,* he'd said to her when she woke him. 'Shush,' she'd replied. *Just shush and go back to sleep.* Close to him, holding him all the night long.

Addie Lacher knew when bad was about to happen. She knew and she did not grieve over it, for it never did any good to whine or to grovel, because it was all God's plan, and there was no use being a coward when God had already decided what was what. She wasn't sure, but she was pretty certain that God didn't like cowards. No one could ever accuse Addie of being a coward.

Still, now, lately, she could almost say that she was afraid. Her dreams had been passing strange in recent weeks. In the past, the things she had seen (*visions*, Preacher Watts had called them) and the dreams she had experienced had always been mild things; things she could hammer out in her mind if she thought about them, but never anything so disturbing as to be frightening unless she thought about the consequences.

For instance, standing on a strange hill (a hill was something else Addie had never seen) and waving to her son and her husband far off down in a valley was not frightening. But dwelling on what it might be like to be without them was a hard and cold thing. Her recent dreams had not been like that at all.

There had been nothing vague about the lizard coming out of the rock. There had been nothing confusing about seeing the great, scaly thing rip and shred meat. There had been nothing opaque about seeing a human head drop from the thing's long, toothy jaws.

Red. Her dreams had been a bright and vibrant red.

Addie knew what alligators were. When she had been very young, there had been lots of alligators in the creeks and ponds around Woodvine. And now that they weren't allowed to be hunted they again dwelled in their old haunts. This thing in her dream was not an alligator. It was much, much too big to be an alligator--even bigger than the fourteen-footer her father and her uncles had killed when she was a girl.

In the first of those disturbing dreams, she had seen the thing come out of the rocks, almost as if the stones were nothing more than eggs. And the birds saw the thing come out of the hard stone, taking wing to places where it could not reach them; they were afraid of it. Then it had stood from where it had appeared from the lichened earth, stretching high above the ground, till its head dwelled amidst the tops of the scraggly pines in the summer heat. Addie rarely dreamed of real places as they truly were. Her dreams were usually puzzles that God gave her to put together in her waking hours.

Ah, but this one was different. Even in her dream she knew that she was seeing a real place, a true place. It was a spot she never had liked; a spot that gave her a queasy feeling whenever she had been there. Even before it looked at her with those glittering green eyes she knew that it had come out of Thirty Acre Rock.

A week later she had dreamed of the old white people. She recognized their faces: people she had seen sometimes in days when she had spent time in Woodvine with Roy. The man's name was Billy, and his wife was Shelley. She would've remembered that even if they had not called to one another in her dream. That had been all to the dream, that time. Two nights later, she saw the house the two lived in, and she saw Davis Ryan with them. Addie liked Davis.

For a white man, he was a decent sort. She remembered that he had taken up for her son when white boys had picked on him, and she remembered that he had given Roy work when he hadn't been able to jobs at the lumber yard during slow times. Even now, he would sometimes bring his pickup out to her cabin to check on her even though he knew the folk from AME Zion stopped by once a week to see about her welfare. Again, that was all there was to the dream.

Billy, Shelley, and Davis at the old couple's house.

When next she dreamed of them, she saw the old man standing by his corn field. He was standing there, staring up at the glistening hulk of studded flesh that reared above him on taloned feet. Quickly, there was movement: jaws opening, closing. Not a spray of red, but something worse--noises; snapping noises, like young, supple pines being bent in two. Then the old woman went, too. Gone, the both of them.

But the worst dream was this:

She dreamed that she was high up, looking down at the earth as if from the treetops. Quietly, she looked about, saw that she was standing in the middle of Thirty Acre Rock. The ground at her feet was bright, and she could see every pebble in contrast of light and shadow; every lichen and sprout was revealed to her. The trees at the edge of the exposed rock were vague, though; it was as if they were smeared strokes of green and brown. Breathing, she could smell something. It was a pleasant smell, as of food to someone who was very hungry. Sniffing, she followed it, moving away from the rock toward the source of that smell. High up, amidst the branches of all but the tallest trees, she floated away, following.

As Addie moved along, she saw that she was in familiar country. There was the road that led down to her cabin. There was the trail that led to her door. Davis Ryan's truck was there, parked at the end of the sandy track that went to her yard. She went down it, looking upon at her house as she had never seen it, seeing blood brown streaks of rust on the tin roof there. And on her house was a sign, a symbol of some kind.

It was as if the sign had been painted in the air, and wasn't truly on the surface of the house. Watching, she saw Davis Ryan pass right through the symbol where it covered her door; he passed right through as if it were not even there. He was running; he was running as fast as he could through the woods to his truck. She turned a bit, watched him go, and did not pursue his little form. There was the symbol and the smell, and the hunger. She dipped toward the house 'and the wall gave way at her touch, sending woody splinters flying into the yard'.

Addie stared at the inside of her house revealed to the outside air, seeing her fireplace in the bright sun, seeing her old rocker tilted on its side, seeing her table broken in half, her couch skewed away from the remaining wall at its rear.

And she saw a tiny, wizened woman looking up at her, looking calmly up from where she hovered so high above looking, in turn, on the old person. She stooped, bringing herself low, closer to the woman, seeing the symbol shrink down until it was a red, red target on the old woman's torso. The smell of food filled her nostrils and it was a good thing to open her watering mouth.

In that instant, she saw that the old woman was she, that the great coiling snake-lizard-thing in her visions was bearing down on her and *that she could not run, could not escape.* Rail-spike teeth came together and she was in their way.

It would have been a good thing if she had awakened then.

She had not. Addie Lacher had seen, as if from some point out of herself, as the gigantic thing had bitten into her. There had been blood, but not much, for it lifted her up, snapped its reptilian head back in a quick motion, tearing her momentarily free of its teeth so that her body slid easily down its terrible throat.

Only then did she awaken.

Since then, Addie had not dreamed much. She had slept some, but restlessly. The forests were horribly quiet. All the birds were gone, and the insects were silent, as if holding their breaths, as if they were hiding in wait for something great. Addie Lacher had not dreamed any more of the thing that resembled a terrible lizard.

She dreamed, instead, of a man. She saw him as he stood at the edge of Thirty Acre Rock, doing something, painting something there, making sounds that were not words.

He was calling that great creature out of the rock; had already done so, she knew. But Addie Lacher couldn't see his face; it was obscured by the tenacious undergrowth that surrounded the Rock; she could not recognize him, could not be sure who he was. In her last dream, (the one she'd had just hours before), she had crept up, through the woods, so that she could make certain of his identity.

Sneaking up to him, she was almost sure.

Unfortunately, he had turned at that moment. And he had spotted her, too, although she had hidden herself well enough so that he could not tell who she was, either.

Addie knew enough to be sure that her time was soon up. She had always known that God would show her before the time came.

But, now, it seemed a cruel thing to have shown her what the dreams had brought.

There was a reason for it, though. She was not fool enough to know that all this had been done for no good reason. The Lord wanted her to tell someone who she had seen in her visions. She had to tell Davis Ryan who it was doing this awful thing. Addie only hoped that she could tell him before it was too late to do anything about it.

Addie didn't want to dream any more. She knew she must; for herself, and for the people of Woodvine. For their souls if for nothing else.

CHAPTER TWELVE

It was almost like a festival.

Arriving at the Wishon farm, Davis and Pat and Michelle had to park Pat's car at the end of the driveway, for the whole of the sandy length was filled with vehicles of every type—it seemed that everyone Sage and his cronies had contacted had come. Despite Davis' concern for the old couple, he was somewhat bitter that so many should come at the call of the man who had done so much damage to the town.

Michelle had insisted on tagging along. She wanted to be nearby to make sure that Davis did not overtax himself as he had done the previous day. "I won't have it," she had told him. So

Davis had allowed her to come, and his cooler was filled not so much with beer as with tea, although Michelle had allowed him the one six pack. Already, he was thinking of popping the top on a can, but he'd wait until he and Pat were ready to trek into the brush on their own before he'd do so.

The three of them got out, feeling the heat blare at them in contrast to the coolness of the car's interior. Pat and Davis toted opposite ends of the full cooler, ice clacking like dry bones as they tromped down the driveway. The growl of Billy's tractor rattled at them as it eased away from the barn, Kiser perched behind the wheel.

As it pulled away, Davis and the others could see that a flatbed wagon had been attached to it, and that the pair of slaughtered cattle had been loaded on. Three other men followed along behind the wagon as Kiser took it across the corn field to the woods where the bodies could be dumped. Even from a distance Davis could smell the bloated, rotting carcasses.

It had been the best thing to move the mess, even if it meant tampering with evidence that a competent investigator might need.

"GBI might've wanted to look at that bull and cow," Davis said.

"GBI? Don't be silly, Davis." Pat said no more as they approached the front porch of the Wishon home.

"You fellows just set that down and let me take care of it," Michelle told the two, pointing to a spot where she wanted the cooler placed. "You'll need to get moving soon, before it gets too hot to get anything done around here."

As Michelle mounted the stairs and went to the front door, it eased open and Red Sage exited, followed by a half dozen men.

Reverend Weller was with them, smiling at everyone, looking tired and worried, nonetheless.

"Ryan," Sage said. "We've been waiting for you to get here so we could get started." He smiled. A subdued chorus of chuckles tagged his statement.

Before Davis could say anything Sage spoke up, calling out in his booming voice to everyone within range. "Alright, fellows! Gather 'round here! We've got a job to do, so it's about time that we get to doin' it."

Men who had been lounging in the shade of trees near the house came up to the porch where Red and the others stood. Women, including Michelle, faded into the house, leaving the men to their business, watching from behind windows and screens. Red waited as they gathered beneath him, and he almost felt like the Red Sage of older times, speaking before committees and associations and clubs, drumming up votes for his assured victories.

He recalled the campaigns, his eyes misting as each memory filed out for inspection. Someone cleared his throat; it sounded like Davis Ryan.

"Excuse me," he said, grinning, "But seeing all of you gathered here like this just made me think that Woodvine isn't as long gone as some would have us believe." He shook his head to toss his hair to the right, out of his eyes. Several exclamations of *Amen* bubbled up from the crowd of old men. As usual, he had them.

"Well," he continued, "I reckon I don't need to tell you why we're all here. If you didn't already know, then you'd probably all be at home watching teevee or sittin' around the breakfast table nibblin' on bacon and eggs. Now, we've got a job ahead of us, and we need to get going on it before it gets too hot, but we'll just keep right on doing it once noon hits, so don't let a little bit of heat scare any of you fellows away.

"Now, we're going to search this entire area around Bill and Shelley's farm until we find out where they may have wondered off to. We know they ain't around the farmhouse or the pasture or the field where Billy planted his fine corn. So what we're going to do is break up into parties, and each party will take a different section around the farm. I reckon we can search as far west as Fanner's Creek, or as far east as the Spur. To the south, I don't see much good in going any further than Goodbread's Swamp, and of course there ain't a whole lot to be accomplished hunting further north than our fair city." He paused while a few chuckled at his little levity.

"Chief Kiser and the others will just commence their search when they're through takin' care of the mess we cleared out of the barn this morning, so that area is taken care of. What we need from here on is about eight groups of four each to light off in different directions to scout out the rest of the search area. Are we in agreement on this, so far?" He scowled down at everyone, daring them to take up a contrary position. No one did, and there was a general murmur of agreement.

"Good," he told them. "What I reckon we can do now is let the Reverend here split us all up into groups so that we can get the job done. But first, I guess we should all just shut up so that he can give this little undertaking a blessing." Red turned toward the house, where Reverend Weller was standing just outside the screened front door. He stepped to the fore, looking down at the gathering.

"Gentlemen. Ladies." He peered into the crowd, looked behind him at the women watching from the house. Far off, he could still hear the muted growl of Billy Wishon's tractor. As if on cue, it ceased its noise. There was only the slight breeze and the occasional throat clearing.

"Dear Lord," he began, "we ask that, as we begin this task of searching for our brother and sister, Bill and Shelley Wishon, that You watch over Your servants as they search for those who need us. And we ask that You guide them all safely and keep them from harm. Also we pray that You have kept Bill and Shelley safe, as we have kept them in our prayers. We ask for Your guidance in finding our friends, and we acknowledge Your compassion for the clear skies and the sun that will show us our way as we search. Dear Lord, we thank Thee.

"Amen."

There was a chorus of voices echoing the minister's last word. The crowd began to splinter into groups that formed about the preacher as he descended the stairs and went to them, counting out men, asking their agreement, sending them on their ways. The reverend was careful, and seemed to remember who got along best with who; he seemed to have made no errors. Finally, Davis Ryan and Pat Wilson were at his side.

"Reverend," Davis addressed him.

"Yes?"

"Before you assign us with anyone, Pat and I would just like to mention that we'd kind of like to strike out on our own." Davis gave the preacher a serious look.

"Why is that, Davis?" Behind them, Red Sage was watching, although he said nothing.

"Well, we've been thinking about it, and we'd just like to have a look around on our own. There are some things we'd kind of like to check on." Groups were already beginning to move away from the farmhouse and into the surrounding woods.

Almost absently, the minister called out to them. "We must all meet back here no later than three! Have you got that?" Men waved and grunted at him, wandering away. He turned back to Davis and Pat.

"What's wrong with going off with Wesley Jarman's group? Where is that you want to search?"

"We just have a few ideas, and we want to take a look-see. That's all." He glared at the preacher.

"It ain't like we're asking your permission, Raymond," Pat said, using the minister's first name. Pat enjoyed calling him by his first name, especially since he knew the preacher didn't like it. They weren't friends.

"I don't see what good it will do to go tramping about on your own, but if it's what you want to do, then go ahead." With a wave of his hand, he turned on his heel and headed back to the house.

"I reckon you and Sage are going to just kind of stay here and coordinate things, huh?" Pat had to smirk at the pair as they stood together on the front porch.

"As a matter of fact, Wilson, that is exactly what Reverend Weller and I are going to do." With that, both headed for the door.

Walking to Pat's car to retrieve their guns, Sage called out to them; an afterthought. "By the way," the yelled. "Where is it that you fellows want to look?" Red stood, hands on hips, thinking he looked like Douglas MacArthur, and waited for the reply.

"We're going to take a look over to Thirty Acre Rock, Red. That's all."

"Why there, of all places? It's a good piece off."

Davis stopped as he neared Pat's car, "Just a feeling, Red! Just a feeling!"

They came out of the woods on a flat expanse of crumbly rock, the air waffling in waves of heat radiating up from the warming stone. Small trees gave way to worn granite in an area roughly the size of a small house. But it was all very flat, with no rise in the land or stones sitting in high relief above the surrounding countryside. To Davis, that had always been the strangest thing about Thirty Acre Rock; it just seemed to be a thin layer of stone lying along the earth, like a scab on a fresh wound. Davis grunted when his boot scrubbed loose pebbles between sole and stone.

Pat and Davis had decided not to walk the old trail that most others took to get to the Rock from the nearest road that paralleled the anomaly. True, the trail wasn't used as much as in days past, but Davis didn't want to bump into anyone. He wanted to snoop undisturbed.

"You ready for one of those beers, Davis," Pat asked.

"Sure. That was pretty sly of you hiding those beers from Michelle in the trunk that way." Davis smiled and reached for the beaded can Pat offered.

"Yeah." He popped the tab on one for himself and tilted it back. Wiping his lips, he continued, "And we might as well polish these off pretty quick, 'cause they aren't going to stay too cold in this little backpack. It's already gettin' hot." He wiped at his forehead and looked over the rock that lay before them. This was merely a tiny smudge of stone, one of dozens that lay like blemishes around the main body of Thirty Acre Rock. Sick looking trees stood all around the exposed granite there.

"Kind of ugly hereabouts," Davis stated. "I never have liked coming here."

"Me, neither. No deer around, and the rabbit hunting is fair in the best years. No quail, either." Pat, always thinking in terms of his hobby.

"Sure, but it's something else about this place. I never have liked it, even when I was a kid."

"I dunno. When I was little, I used to like coming out to the Rock to go swimming. Kind of cool in the main pool there in the middle, sometimes." Pat squinted, considering his youth.

"Not me." Condensation trickled through his fingers as he turned the can bottom to the sky. He swallowed, belched.

"What do you mean?"

"I never did like swimming there. Even if it was cooler in that spot where Fanner's Creek cuts through the rock, the walk out and back was hotter than Hell, and I always got sweaty goin' back across." It was true.

"Never bothered me, but I know a few who felt the same as you. My dad never did like comin' out here, and he didn't like me comin' out here, either." Again, he smiled, thinking of his younger days. It had been a while since he'd thought of his father: big, gruff old fellow; stout from working in the lumber yard; old too soon, and gone.

"Been long since you were here?"

Pat considered for a moment, trying to recall the last time he had walked across this weathered rock. "Yeah...gimme a minute."

He paused, surprised at not being able to remember. "Christ, Davis, it's been a long time..."

"How 'bout 1984?" Davis peered at his old friend.

"'84?" He thought, trying to remember. "Shit, Davis, I think you're right!"

"Back when I was runnin' against Red the last time."

"Back the last time we had a marauding bear around here! Shit, yes!" Pat gazed around, awed that it had been that long since he had set foot in this area. "Yeah! Old Dan Morris had some of his hogs killed. An' while Red's old buddies were baggin' that bear, me an' some of the others were trackin' over this way with the hounds. Sixteen years. Shit."

"Strange business, that." Davis reached over and crammed the empty can into Pat's pack and withdrew a full one to replace it. Escaping gas hissed out as he popped the top.

"Yeah. Remember how Dan's redbones were just running around the woods here not finding nothin'. They were mainly just chasin' 'coons and not gettin' any sign of bear. Those dogs weren't worth a damn that day."

"Except for Arthur Jarmon's bird dog."

"Damndest thing, wasn't it? All those good, strong redbones could do was chase their tails, and that bird dog strikes a trail." He chuckled. "Led us on a chase, huh?"

"Yeah. I still ain't figured that out. She was leading us after something, but the trail just died out."

"At Fanner's Creek, there. Right where it cuts through the Rock. Whatever it was must've crossed the creek, or went in, and

Art's dog just lost the scent. That was one frustrated dog."

"And Red and his buddies ended up shootin' that scrawny bear over on the other side of town. I never have thought that little bear killed Dan's hogs. He was just too damned little. Hardly a year old, that one."

"But there weren't any more hogs killed, was there?"

"No." Davis had to admit it. "And ol' Red went and won him another election on account of that.

"Hell, Davis, you know he always had a trick up his sleeve to beat anybody who ran against him. Hell! He prob'ly killed those hogs himself and bought him a yearling bear somewhere and let it out so that him and his buddies could kill it!" He paused for a moment, reflecting, thinking about the old politician. "Remember that guy that ran against him back in...'74. What was that fella's name?"

"Jerry Coye. Nice guy." Davis turned the warming can of beer to his lips and finished it off in one, long slug. He burped again.

"But ol' Red was right about him all along, huh?"

"What do you mean?"

"He kept sayin' all during the campaign that Coye was just here kind of fly-by-night, and that he'd leave after a while.

Didn't wait around though, did he? Not even for the election."

Davis kept his mouth shut. He had liked Coye, had gotten to know him fairly well in the time the man had spent in Woodvine.

And he never had understood how Coye could have just taken off as he had. If ever he could've suspected Sage of doing the worst, it was during that time.

But Coye's car had gone, too, along with everything of value in his house; and he had emptied his bank account before taking off for parts unknown. No one had ever heard from him again, but no one ever considered foul play. Still, Davis had often wondered what Sage had done to make the man light out like that.

"Red must have found some dirt somewhere, and he had threatened to reveal it if the man didn't leave; at least, that's how Davis had always figured it.

"He couldn't have beat Red that year. Not with Red stirrin' things up over those colored children. Search parties again, huh? Kind of like now. We never did find those kids."

"Never did. Looked every damned where for those children. Everywhere." Davis recalled the long searches, tramping about trackless woods, poking about the banks of Fanner's Creek, plunging into the swamps as he and others had looked for the kids.

And nobody had seemed to be more concerned and condescending than Red Sage. 'Red's huntin' for those poor nigra children like they were his own,' people had said. 'What a good, Christian man,' the word had gone. Red had won another election.

"Well," Pat said, "we better get lookin'. The Rock's a big place." He took a step, grinding gritty earth underfoot.

"Let's get to it."

They pushed across the bit of stone and continued on to the mass of Thirty Acre Rock.

"You think we'll find anything way out here?" Pat reached out and shoved at a dead branch that would have scratched at his face. Dry twigs and old, reddened pine thatch crackled underfoot.

"I don't know, Pat. But it ain't too far from here to Billy's place, and if any hoodlums from Martinsville were prowlin' around out this way, then they were probably out here messin' around the Rock in the first place. You know how rowdy kids can be.

"They might've come out here to see the Rock, or to get drunk and go swimmin' in Fanner's Creek, and then they just stumbled on Billy and Shelley's farm. And then, maybe they decided to kill his cattle and one thing led to another. Hell, Pat. I don't know. I don't know how other people's minds work. Why would anybody want to hurt somebody like Billy and Shelley, anyway?"

Davis veered to the left, making his way around a patch of brambles and blackberry thicket. Stray thorns scraped at his pants leg, and he held his rifle tight to his chest, its bore aimed skyward. Ahead, he could see clear sky where there were no trees: Thirty Acre Rock.

Almost to the main section of the Rock, Davis put out his right hand to halt Pat. "Hush," he said. His voice was harsh in the hot silence.

Pat said nothing; he merely stood in place like a good tracker and waited; sweat tickled it way down the sides of his face.

Carefully, Davis moved forward until he was at the edge of where the anemic woods gave way to stubborn rock. He knelt there, lay his gun on the pine needles, and he quietly parted the screen of oak limbs that were in his way. He peered out at the Rock.

Again, he couldn't help but think of the Rock as nothing but a great, old scab that lay over a terrible wound in the Earth.

After a while, Pat crept up to his friend. "What is it, Davis," he whispered, at last.

On the Rock, the sun was playing over a pale expanse of lichened stone. Here and there, from ancient cracks, spears of bear grass and brooms edge poked up, creating dark lines of contrast in the unremarkable feature. A hundred yards away Davis could see where the Rock was cut by Fanner's Creek; a slope led down to the water that he couldn't quite view. There was no movement out there. No lizard flicked from shadow to shadow. No dragonfly darted up from where the creek sluggishly flowed. No birds preened in nearby trees.

"Nothing," Davis said. "There's nothing out there."

Moving, Pat pushed on through the barrier of little red oaks that stood in their way; leaving Davis crouched in the warm shadows. "Well, then, let's take a look out here and see what we can see."

Davis followed, walking out from his hidden spot, scanning the rough granite for signs. For what he was searching, he did not know, precisely. Just something that showed that someone had recently been out here. "You take the south end," Davis suggested.

"I'll head up this way."

"Okay," Pat agreed. For two hundred yards in almost every direction there was nothing to block visibility. There were no features to hide anything, no trees to mask or conceal. They split up, moving farther apart as they searched.

After an hour on the east side they found a shallow spot and waded across Fanner's Creek, splashing quickly to the other side.

The water was tanned, slightly brown from the acidic earth it passed through in the swamp a short distance away; but pure for all its color. On the other side they continued their search, and after another hour and with no beer remaining, they conceded defeat. They had found nothing but the whitening rock that spread everywhere. Even the faded remnants of bleached beer cans and rotting paper plates were not to be found. It seemed as if it had been an awfully long time since anyone had chosen to have a picnic on Thirty Acre Rock. There just seemed to be nothing there.

Gripping his rifle in one hand and wiping at his perspiring forehead with the other, Pat was ready to surrender. "It's past two," he told Davis. "I think we'd better head on back."

"Yeah. I reckon you're right. Let's go on."

With the sun heating the surface of the Rock, with no wind to diminish the temperature, the two went back toward Pat's waiting car, leaving Thirty Acre Rock to itself.

On a small irregularity of the Rock, a wriggling arm that jutted into a scrubby copse of sickly pines, the pair did not see the flakes of red paint that had been inadvertently left there. They did not see the rough leather patches, strange symbol hastily embossed on each that lay wrapped in a cloth sack, all stashed carefully beneath close grown palmettoes. They missed it entirely, going back to the Wishon farm and to the others.

CHAPTER THIRTEEN

By three in the afternoon the whole of the search party had returned to the Wishon home. While the men compared notes and freed themselves from ticks and beggars lice, the women prepared sandwiches and bowls of beans and potato salad for all. As before, the atmosphere was as that of a festival, and but for the fact that every face was lined with age and no children's voice cracked the general murmur of conversation, it was almost as if the town were still bustling and alive. People came again and again to Red Sage to impart information or to ask advice. The whole situation ground on Davis' nerves like sand in gears.

When the sun had begun to descend toward the treetops, paper plates and disposable cups were tossed into and bound up in plastic bags. The small messes caused by the gathering were cleaned, and the orders of the Wishon home were made right. The dirty clothes that Billy and Shelley had left in hampers and on the bedroom floor were washed and dried; Billy's barn was shoveled clear of the remains of the rotting animals, his tractor was replaced in its own stall, and the doors of the barn were closed up tight and locked. As shadows lengthened and darkness was a thing that loomed large and real, the crowd began to disperse; car engines revved, trucks muttered gassily, and wheels left clouds of sand in their wakes.

Although disappointed that nothing was found, that no clue as to the Wishons' whereabouts was located, the people of Woodvine seemed strangely happy, at ease with themselves as they had not been in a long time. And as each of them moved off to their own cars to be away to their homes back in town, all stopped to say a word and to shake the hand of Red Sage--as if he were once again their mayor; as if no one recalled the rumors that his cooperation with county politicians had caused the disasters that had killed the town. Those questions were forgotten in the rush of being useful, of doing something.

Finally, all were gone save Red and his minister-in-tow and his old crony, Kiser. And Davis, Pat, and Michelle lingered in the Wishon house, puttering, putting things to order. Then the old squad car was away, and only Davis and his two remained.

Only then did Davis say what had been itching at the back of his mind for several hours.

"You know," Davis said, pointing through the forests that grew behind Billy's house. "Addie Lacher lives about a mile as the crow flies through those woods."

"Think she's seen anything?" Michelle asked.

"I think I'll go and ask her."

Pat looked wistfully at the others. "Damn," he said. "I didn't even know that old woman was still alive."

"Oh, she is," Davis said. "She is. Too damned stubborn to die."

CHAPTER FOURTEEN

The night before, she had dreamed of a top; a great, spinning top that whirled and whirled all around, looping about the floor, smashing into walls. She woke up.

Addie didn't know what the dream meant; it didn't make sense to her, and she felt small, somehow; as if she were not up to the task that had been presented to her. But today Davis Ryan was going to come to see her, so she couldn't worry herself terribly wondering what that dream meant. For after all, there had been the other dreams; they were much more disturbing. And she knew all too well what they meant.

She had dreamed again of the man at Thirty Acre Rock. Addie wanted to go there herself. She wanted nothing more than to go to Thirty Acre Rock so that she could walk about that awful expanse of granite and see what was so terrible about it. Again in her dream she had crept close to the man, trying to see what he was doing there before he saw her.

It was obvious now that he was aware, at times, of her presence. Addie wondered if knowing she could see him was disturbing his own dreams. She hoped that were so.

The last time she had seen him, she had crawled to the edge where the trees grew right up to the rock; where Fanner's Creek poked out of the forest and played its way across the granite.

Behind the cover of big oak leaves she had peeked at the man—she at least knew that he was a white man, now--and tried as hard as she could to see his face. But his back had been to her, and she could tell nothing of his identity from his clothes. He was dressed in dark pants, and his weathered white hands poked from the cuffs of a simple, blue shirt. He wore leather street shoes not meant for tramping about in the woods or out on Thirty Acre Rock.

As she had watched him, she saw that he was doing something with paint that he was drawing something on the ground, and on the surfaces of patches of leather he drew out of a cloth bag. He had made a kind of sign--like a letter, only 'not' a letter—on the earth. He had drawn something with the same red paint on the patches from the bag, too. Then the sounds had come out of his mouth.

Addie had to say they were sounds, for they were not words; rather, they were awful guttural noises such as she had never heard, even in her worst nightmares. Dwelling upon it, she had decided that it wasn't so much the voice that was uttering the sounds so much as it was the utterances themselves; they seemed to send shivers through her each time the man spoke them. After that, his shoulders tensed, and she had known that he sensed her, then.

For a while, he pretended that she was not there, but she knew better. Addie realized that he was only feigning ignorance of her. Little by little, she edged away from where she hid, trying not to step upon the dry leaves and twigs underfoot. It was only because she had already begun to retreat that he did not catch her when he suddenly turned to race her way.

Addie knew that if he caught her, even in her dream, that she would be killed. Knowing that, feeling it, she stayed out of his way until she was able to awaken, being silent and remaining hidden; her only defense, for she was much too old to even think about trying to run from someone so obviously more robust than she.

The worst of it had been that though she had known she was dreaming and wanted nothing more than to be awake, she could not rouse herself from the state in which she found herself. She had been trapped until a beam of sunshine had pierced the panes of her bedroom window and the shaft of light had awakened her, hurting her eyes. It had been a wonderful pain, though, just to wake up before she was caught.

Still, she had not seen his face.

She really had nothing to tell Davis Ryan when he came. Nothing, at all. She could not expect him to believe that she could see the future that she could see, in her mind, things that happened many miles away even as they occurred. Perhaps, she hoped, there would be some kind of vision, a realization...

With his truck parked a quarter of a mile away, Davis walked up the sandy trail that led to Addie Lecher's house. The trail was well worn and Davis could see the tracks Addie had left there in her latest journey to and from the small garden she tended near the spot he had parked his pickup. He well knew the schedule of her weekly visitor from Martinsville, recalling that it had been four days since the last volunteer had come from the AME Zion Church there. More than enough time for her to have been victimized by the same criminals who had done God knew what at the Wishon farm. Davis didn't like the idea of walking up the path unarmed, but he left his pistol in the cab of his truck since he didn't want to alarm the old woman with the sight of a man approaching her house with a loaded gun. Addie knew him, but it had been weeks since he had visited her.

When he was less than a dozen steps from her front door Davis saw her sitting in her rocker on the small porch that fronted the house. She rocked easily back and forth, watching him as he came near. In a simple blue dress she sat, waiting for the white man to come to her. When he got to the bottom step, she finally spoke.

"Davis Ryan." She smiled at him, flashing the dentures the church had bought for her the year before.

"Hello, Ms. Lacher." Davis smiled back at her. "I haven't been out this way in a while, so I thought that I'd stop by and see how you were doing."

"Well, I'm doing just fine, young man." She halted her rocking for a moment. "Why don't you come on up and have a seat here," she said, indicating the straight backed cane chair she had brought out of her kitchen, knowing he was coming.

"Yes, ma'am. I think I will." He came up the steps, clumping over to sit next to her. Breathing in, he could smell the accumulated years of which the cane chair reeked: layers of scents; strange, but not unpleasant. Davis gazed over at the old woman, her hair still black despite her ninety-plus years. Her face was terribly old though, wrinkled flesh making folds that nearly hid her eyes and that hung like flaps upon her neck. He supposed she really should be in a home somewhere, but she'd so

far talked her AME Zion benefactors out of such action.

"Any other reason you might be out this way, Davis Ryan? It *has* been a while." She watched him, waiting, feeling him out.

Davis leaned forward in the chair, rubbed at his face and wondered how he should put it. He didn't want to needlessly alarm the woman, but he wanted to ask her some things. How could he do it without frightening her?

"Don't hold your tongue on account of me," she told him.

Addie wanted to just come out and ask him about the Wishon couple; but if she did that, then he would just become suspicious like most white men would. And that was not at all what she wanted. No.

Davis Ryan was her last chance to tell somebody what was going on. If only she knew more. If only she knew exactly what was happening, and who it was doing it. "You've got something bothering you."

"Yes. And I don't know how to put it without worrying you,

Ms. Lacher." There was a strange, strained smile on his face; the genuine concern painted there made Addie like him all the more.

"Don't you concern yourself with worrying me, Davis. I'm ninety-three years old, and there just is not a whole lot that I have not heard of. You go right ahead and tell me whatever you please." She, too, leaned forward in her seat, as if the two were sharing some terrible gossip.

"Have you *seen* anything in the last week?"

God, if only I could tell him! "Such as...?"

"Well, like any strange persons messin' around here."

"Like who, for instance?"

"I'm not sure. But, some kids, maybe. You know, maybe some like those white kids that threw rocks and tore up people's yards a few years back."

"No. I can't say that I've seen any young hoodlums away out here in the woods, Mr. Ryan. No kids, at all.

"In fact," she continued, "the church doesn't even send a young buck out to see to me anymore. They have to send old Mr. Dugan. He's a deacon, you know." She didn't want him suspecting some poor black kid of anything. "Why do you ask?" *Now.*

"We've just had some strange things happening in Woodvine."

Davis cleared his throat, trying to decide how to continue.

"What kinds of things, Davis?"

"Do you remember the Wishons? Got a farm..."

"Not much more than a mile from here," she finished, halting Davis in midsentence. "Bill and Shelley Wishon. Two kids. At least they used to have two children."

"Yes. That's them." He breathed out through his nose, thinking.

"What's happened to them?"

"Well..."

"They're missing, aren't they?" She had to say it. What good would it do to feign ignorance?

Davis leaned back in the chair as if struck. He stared at the old woman, suspicions filing one after the other, all but spilling out of the lips he had now clamped so tightly over his teeth.

"How did you know that?" He finally got it out.

"It was either that, or someone killed them," she said, feeling strange, wanting to blurt out all that she knew and all that she suspected.

"Ms. Lacher...do you know something? I..." He stared at her, his eyes wide; and Addie could see the fatigue in them, on his face, in the way that he moved. "Do you know something that you're not telling me? You're not trying to hide something are you?"

A sadness came over the old woman then. She could see the fear on him, in the way that he held his body rigid in the chair, in the twitching of his thin lips, in the perspiration that suddenly cropped like pinprick wells on his pale forehead. *White folk: they were all the same--even the better ones.* And, too, as if the delayed shock of a distant thunderbolt, she saw the redness of his eyes, the fatigue in his demeanor she should have already noticed.

"You look tired, Mr. Ryan. Something is bothering you. Something bad," she said.

"I haven't slept," he told her. "I haven't been able to sleep well at all since this thing with Bill and Shelley. Nightmares," he told her.

Addie's guts froze. A gallon of ice water was poured over her old heart, into her stomach, onto her lungs. *It could be Davis!* The horror of the realization almost caused her to faint. *It could be Davis Ryan!* And she was here, alone, with him. And he was pressing her for information, and she had almost given it to him. All he would need to do was what he felt he must to stop the one who might know what he was about. *Alone, alone, alone.*

"Ms. Lacher? Are you alright?" Davis stood and went to her, placing his right hand on the angular shoulder beneath the blue fabric. She felt terribly frail under the press of his strong hand, like a framework of balsawood.

The old woman blinked, made herself peer deep into the white man's eyes despite the fear she felt, despite this new and awful suspicion. She had to do it. Looking, she could see only concern in his brown eyes. There was nothing of hatred. There was no reciprocal fear in those eyes. *It can't be Davis*, she reasoned. But the suspicion would not go away, no matter how she tried.

Sighing, Addie spoke. "I'm just fine," she said. "All this talk of missing people...it just has me on edge is all." She gazed back into Ryan's face. "And I know how you white people can be. I don't want you suspecting anyone from the church of doing anything to the Wishons. I won't have it just because some good people see to my needs," she told him.

"No, no, Ms. Lacher! I didn't mean it like that, at all! I swear!" Davis stood, knowing he had upset Addie; it was exactly what he had not wanted to do. "That thought never crossed my mind, I promise!"

"I just know how you people can be," she repeated.

"Yes, ma'am." There was no use in trying to deny it; in trying to contradict what he knew was going through her mind. A woman who had seen people killed for the color of their skin was no one to argue such a point with. "All I wanted to know was whether or not you have seen anything suspicious out here. That's all I was wondering about."

"I'm feeling tired," she suddenly said, rising from the rocker, revealing the threadbare cushion of orange cloth beneath her, pale batting trying to poke through. "I think I'm just going to go back in a get some rest." Addie turned toward the open door.

"Are you going to be alright?"

"I'll be fine. When you get to be my age, you have to rest a bit. That's all."

"Do you need anything," Davis asked her, feeling awful, having done precisely what he had intended not to do. "I can make a call for you back at the house, if you want."

"No, no," she said. "Don't you bother anyone. I'm fine." She smiled for him to prove her point. "I'm just going to lie down for a while."

"I can come back out later," he said. "Or tomorrow, if you'd like."

She stepped under the threshold. "If you feel you have to."

Standing just inside her home she watched Davis edge off the porch, moving slowly, feeling the clumsy silence. Beyond, a breeze was moving through the pines, making soft noises as branches sighed against the wind. The sun darkened a bit as Ryan stepped down to the sandy earth.

"Wind's coming up," he said, trying to break the tension.

Addie watched him crane his neck skyward, saw his graying hair droop against his ears. Shadows moved across his face as unseen clouds hid the sun. "Might be a storm coming," he said. A stronger gust snapped at the nearby trees, seemingly to punctuate his statement.

All at once Addie thought of her dream: the top spinning and bouncing about her little house. "A storm?" She whispered it, and Davis didn't even hear the words.

"I'll stop by tomorrow," he told her, waving and retreating down the sandy path.

Standing in her doorway, Addie saw a shadow from beneath one of her big pines detach itself from where it ought to be. The darkness moved away from the pine and covered Ryan as he faded around a bend in the path. She blinked and the shadow was where it ought to be.

As she sobbed, she prayed, asking God not to make her dream. She knew he would, though.

CHAPTER FIFTEEN

With the winds playing about the tops of the trees, he stood in the center of the spot that had been shown to him so many years before. Strange, now, how he could feel the vibration that rang up from the rock in never ending waves. It was almost a ticklish sensation that nibbled at the balls of his feet and shook at his shinbones.

No one else could feel it; it was something that was reserved for him and for no one else. At least since he had killed the strange little man who had revealed it all to him. The small, foreign stranger had felt it, had called it a 'power point', had said that there were damned few of them on the Earth, that this one had been untouched since its creation.

The old man stood on the top of the Rock and thought about that. *Since its creation*, no one had meddled with this place.

Oh, people came out here from time to time to see and to dawdle; but no one had ever tapped it for what it possessed. Of course no one, or damned few, knew what could be done here, what lay in wait here, what could so easily be called up.

Calling. That, too, had been something the little foreigner had shown him. It was so simple, really. So damned simple. All you had to do was know the secret that no one else knew and that no one else would use even if they knew it. Dwelling on things past, he considered that the strange man had only shown him the secret because he felt that the showing would save his life, would gain him freedom from the confines of the bare cell that Woodvine had called its jail back in those pre-war years. Foolish little man.

All dark and swarthy like that, he should have known that he would be mistaken for a nigger, that his strange, babbling accent would mark him as an outsider with no one to turn to for help.

Ah, but he had thought that he could bargain his way out of a bad situation. The only trouble had been that he had bargained with the wrong person. He should have chosen one of the idiots who may have wielded enough power to free him without causing undue attention.

Kiser could have done it, but the little man had seen at once that the police chief was nothing but a savage brute who knew little more than how to curse and use his nightstick. And there had been a host of others who could have freed him with minimum amount of fussing. It would have been simple then to have shown that person what he had to offer, and then he could have been on his way; or he could have used what he knew to get himself out of trouble, to eliminate whomever he wished.

Instead, though, he had seen the tall, robust man who had come to the cell to view him, to see the strange curiosity that had wandered into Woodvine. The little fellow had taken one look and had seen authority and cunning written there, had decided that if he were to deal, then this was surely the one with whom he would do it.

The trouble had been, though, that he had underestimated just how ruthless Red Sage truly was.

Kneeling on the warm stone that only stubbornly gave up the heat it had absorbed all during the hot day, Sage drew the Sign on the pebbled surface. The Sign was quite pleasing to the eye once you got used to it, once you had utilized it a time or two. He recalled the first time he had actually seen the symbol embossed on a small patch of cowhide the foreigner had shown him. Back then, the thing had alarmed him, had *disturbed* him somehow.

Thinking about it, he couldn't quite recall what his first impression had been; it had simply been that there had been something about it that had seemed to itch at his mind, had bothered him almost to the point of repulsion when he had first seen it.

With firm, careful strokes, he took the brush and red paint and placed the symbol atop the Rock. It was quite simple, actually. Just a few curves, a trio of angles, a thickness here, a narrowing of crimson there. And the thoughts. One had to exercise the proper thoughts to get it done correctly. He speculated, sometimes, that it was the thoughts that mattered most. Not the symbol, not the words that had to be uttered later; but the thoughts, the condition of one's mind as the Sign was made. That, he felt, was what he excelled at. That, he felt, was what had awed the dark-skinned stranger and had been the basis of the stranger's mistake: he had just simply not realized who he was dealing with.

As in other things, Red Sage had a talent for this. A final stroke and he was done, the sign was completed on the stone, a red obscenity drawn for his eyes only. There was a growing lust building in Red Sage as he tossed aside the frayed brush, spattering crimson paint across the ground. There was a burning thirst building in him as he felt *words* clawing to get out of his brain.

Standing, he gazed down at the thing he had made upon the Earth. It seemed to hover above the stone, a thing of three dimensions and not of two. Now there was only the calling to be made, and it would be done. Something fairly shrieked to be let out of him, out of his mind, down to his lungs, spewed from his mouth. He did not wait.

About him, the wind blew in increasing gusts; trees twisted, dancing crazily, leaves rattling, air whining and keening through the green, green needles of the pines. Darkness was upon him, light having fled. And he knew that the light had fled from him and from nothing else. He had the power. He wielded it. God was afraid of him. A noise gurgled up from his guts, out of his throat. "Hhhhhhhhh...."

For an eternal instant all was still. The wind seemed to cease its blowing. It was as if Existence had stopped, as if all time had ceased to flow, to halt what Red Sage was doing; or, if not to stop him, then at least to delay him.

Explosion.

Thunder like no thunder.

Air rushing out into vacuum, screaming into void.

The Rock gave up that which it held in trust to the one who knew how to retrieve. The World was what screamed; it screamed, admitting that which should ever remain at bay, that which should only claw and tear, wanting in but never gaining entrance.

The thunder stopped. Red Sage stood in his place and laughed at it. He laughed and laughed and laughed.

Above him, no more than fifty feet away, out from the ancient granite that had lain for a Jurassic duration, was what he had called. Armored skin glistened magnificently in what remained of light. Great, clawed feet splayed atop Thirty Acre Rock, talons scraping soundlessly, points threatening the stone. Twin supple pillars of flesh supported the mass of the reddish body, a great tail like a third leg completing stability, curling and twisting heavily in the night. Lungs with ten times the capacity of a man's heaved, moving the hill that was its breast. Its vast torso twitched there as the called thing began to move, raising up its gigantic, terrible head on a neck suited for such a task. Slowly, slowly, jaws creaked wide, revealing teeth that showed like ivory swords in the tarry night. Nostrils that were wide enough to hide a heavyweight's fists gaped, sucking, questing for scent.

Straing eyes, glowing like polished glass, surveyed this tiny world.

Red Sage watched the thing and was not afraid of it.

For, called by the Sign, it would seek, in turn, that which was marked by the Sign.

The Sign the old man had planted in places of his choosing.

The search party had been such a grand idea. It had made easy marks of all he chose to destroy.

He tried to recall everyone he had marked, slipping an etched leather oblong here, another one there; some in cars, some in pockets, one in some woman's purse (he wasn't even sure whose). There had really not been any animosity involved in it; in fact, it had mostly been happenstance and opportunity that dictated who was chosen. Toward the end, when everyone was leaving in droves, he had to admit that he'd even lost track of many who had been slipped his little gifts. He doubted most would even notice the damned things.

But he had done his best to mark one person. Sage had done as well as he could to make sure that Davis Ryan would soon be out of his hair. If Red was to do this last thing for Woodvine, he had to do it and do it quickly, before there could be any outside interference, for as great as this thing was, he was not certain that it could not be killed. And Ryan suspected something, suspected it enough that he had even been of a mind to search Thirty Acre Rock, and Sage could not have that.

That was why he had placed one small patch in Pat Wilson's car, and another in the bottom of that cooler they had conveniently left on the Wishons' front porch. He had chosen Ryan just as he had chosen first the Wishons' cattle, then Billy and Shelley themselves, to test himself, to *stretch his wings*, so to speak.

As he had used the secret more and more of late, he had begun to see and know things that otherwise would have remained hidden to him. It was his dreams; the use of the secret was affecting them. In those dreams he had foreseen a problem, and in his sleep he was troubled by someone lurking just out of his sight. He was fairly certain that it had been Davis Ryan dogging his heels in those dreams, and he had wanted nothing more than to catch him and kill him with his bare hands. Those dreams had disturbed him, had left him with the intolerable impression that he would not be able to complete his mission. But those dreams had also spurred him to act.

He was relatively certain that Ryan would not last until daybreak when the beast would return to the Rock.

In the night, he stood and listened as the thing above him breathed in, sniffing, trying to decide at which target to strike. He watched as it suddenly froze, its tail locking in place, jutting out from its giant's body in a horizontal line above the ground. With a display of amazing power, it bounded across the lichened granite, moving tons in long, fluid steps, fading into the blackness of trees.

Toward Woodvine.

CHAPTER SIXTEEN

He didn't know what he was doing there; he really didn't. In his entire life he had never been one to do things spontaneously.

In all ways he had been a thoughtful sort; at least in the way that he composed his own life. That's why Raymond Weller couldn't quite reason what could have possibly possessed him to come here, of all places, and now, of all times.

It was dark, quite dark, and there was no moon to light the way. Only star shine squinted down what illumination there was to be had. Only star shine showed him dark angles and deep pools of shadow that had once been his church. Alone, he stood beside his car and looked up at the steepled building, recalling times when so many of Woodvine's people had flocked there. A wind blew up, gusting again, raking the nearby oaks and shaking green leaves from branches before they were ready to let go. The wind was almost cool on him, and he merely stood, remembering more.

Reverend Weller recalled days when the church had been full, when every pew had been filled to capacity, when there had been talk of building a new church to hold all of the growing membership. But that had been in the days when things were fine; when the town was healthy. That had been in days when everyone came to him for advice and for help.

Red Sage had often come to him for help. Whenever it was campaign time, that was when Sage was there the most. "Give me your support, Raymond. Can I count on you again for an endorsement? I sure could use all those votes! Heh heh."

Heh heh. Another gust rushed up, feeling with soft, insistent fingers at Weller's starched shirt, at his collar, seeking entrance. The warmth of his Pontiac beckoned, but nostalgia had the best of him. There was the old church standing dark and silent in front of him; he heard it calling with memories bursting at its seams, memories to bring smiles by the truckload, tears by the barrelful. He had to go to it, dark as it was.

Dark, old friend. But I know you like I know myself. I know every inch of you, every aisle, every hallway, every closet and room and chamber. I know you. Going up the walkway, he did not stumble on broken paving stones, each of which he knew by heart.

He did not fear a misstep.

The keys jingled in his hand as he drew them out. A new gust of wind drowned the lone, tiny sound; drowned it, picked it up and carried it through the trees. He shoved the keys back into his pocket. His fingers encountered something tough and unyielding there. *What is this?* He drew it out: some rectangular section of stiff material he could see; but it was too dark to make out any detail. *Now how in the world did this end up in my own pocket,* he mused. He decided that he must have merely picked it up with something else, some change, perhaps, when he had been at the Wishon farm. Stuffing it back into his pocket, he went into the church.

Squeaking, the door swung outward fairly easily. The wind tried to snatch it open, but Weller held tight and did not let that happen. Stepping, he pulled the door shut behind him. He was inside.

And how the memories flooded back. He loved the memories. They were his only solace now that he was old and alone, his family long gone, no wife or children to call to his side, no congregation to gather 'round him in these final years. But he had his memories, mostly stored here in this old, aging building, although the structure itself was bare but for the browning pews and fading velvet cushions waiting for worshippers who would never again arrive. Never. It was all over and done with.

The old building still smelled like a church, though. There was that smell of good wood and clean carpet, and a touch of pulp, of aging paper. There were still Bibles and hymnals in the pockets behind each pew, also waiting for hands that would never touch worn bindings, never turn another dog-eared page. Walls reared above polished floors, rafters hung above dusty seats, windows stood in fading walls. And none of it ever to feel again the weight of people coming and going, of voices singing, lifting up tunes to Heaven and to God.

Sobbing, Raymond Weller walked slowly up the eastern aisle, making his way toward the podium where he had given so many sermons. More than a thousand sermons, he reckoned, and all from that one little lectern that Asa Stahl had built for him so many, many years gone. Burying himself in the memories, Weller did not hear the wind outside as it built; he did not note the leaves that came up from the forest floor to fly at the church, there to clatter noisily. He was lost in sweet misery.

At the front of the sanctuary, where he had stood so many times to speak to his congregation, he lingered to stare at the podium. He could see himself there, his great Bible opened, at his fingertips, the people sitting and watching, waiting for the words. Perhaps, he thought, he should give a sermon to himself.

Perhaps he needed to do that. He passed the lectern, going up four carpeted steps, across the raised podium to a door that had probably not been opened in years. He went through it, amazed that the hinges barely protested.

He went down a short hallway, more shadowed than even the sanctuary had been, and moved along walls that he knew were marked with the dark fingerprints left by children. Turning to his left, he reached out and touched the door that led to what had been the nursery. Remembering, he could hear the strident calls of preschoolers, the yelps of toddlers, the screams of yowling infants. He had always loved children. That love of youngsters had been one of the reasons he had heard the call from God to become a minister. More than anything else, he missed the children.

God must have stranded him in this dying town full of old people to punish him for the things he had done. And he had done much to atone for. He hoped he would pay the price in what was left of his life, and not be punished thereafter.

Why did I do it? Why did I let myself be used?

He could blame no one but himself. Red Sage had not twisted his arm, had not threatened him. Sage had merely tempted him, had offered the prizes for Weller's corruption. Raymond was merely weak when he should have been strong. *Come with me, Raymond. Together, we run this town! You know that.*

With his hand on the doorknob, he found he could not go into the room. He wasn't sure he could stand the residue of the children that remained inside. The chalkboard still had a Sunday school lesson scrawled there, written by Mary Gray, perhaps, and some of the children she had always volunteered to keep while parents listened to sermons or gathered to talk in the churchyard.

Weller dropped his hand, turned on his heel, and he retreated down the black hallway to the sanctuary.

Opening the door, he walked across the podium to the lectern. Outside, the wind was kicking up a fuss, tossing debris at the dust grayed windows; waves of leaves broke against the church. Branches raked at the whitewashed walls, and Weller at last was startled out of his nostalgia. He looked up, glancing at the great windows that faced the forest. Out there, the ground thumped as something fell against the earth. Again. Again. The wind actually screamed, whistling in through gaps in the church. Stuff scuttled atop the roof.

The thumping noise came again, closer. It was repeated. At first, Weller thought that the sound must be that of toppling trees. He thought about leaving, of going home. The wind cracked tree limbs: rifle shot noises that startled him. Like something huge approaching, the thumping noise continued, grew in intensity. Weller could actually feel the church vibrating at each concussion. His car was just outside the door. He would leave. Now. A bad storm was coming.

Something filled the window that faced the woods. Even in the black night he could see that something had moved in front of that window, blotting it. Something that moved.

"Dear God," he said.

Above the howling wind Weller heard the sound: a great inhalation, as of some hound snuffling for scent. And then...

The window exploded inward, glass shattering, spinning through the air in glittering arcs. Some of the sharp edges struck him, cut his face. But he did not feel it, could only scream as the wall of the church was pushed aside, pine clapboard peeled down like paper cards. Weller saw a leg push through, clawed feet stamping down on the floor of his church, caving it in. A head jutted in, *something had to bend down to get gain admittance*! Weller screamed once more.

Gripping the lectern with his old hands, the jaws had to shear right through the old wood as the thing bit and lifted Weller up. With its great tongue, it spat out the splinters before swallowing the meat.

Turning about, its massive tail whipped, smashing pews into matchsticks, exiting through the wide hole it had torn in the building. The Scent was everywhere. It had to hunt it all down.

Empty, the shattered church shook less and less as the plodding steps retreated.

CHAPTER SEVENTEEN

Clouds flew in, blown by strange winds. And rain came, falling in great sheets that battered at houses, slashing like thin claws, gusts of air the paws that wielded them. It was an unusual storm, coming out of nowhere to pound the county, sparing most of the towns its fury; merely a potent threat.

Save for Woodvine. For Woodvine, it was no threat, frightening in its intensity.

But it hid the true horror from the ones Sage had not marked. The storm spared that group the insanities of the night.

After leaving the Wishon farm, the sun descending behind the pines, Mary Childress had sat beside her husband in the back seat of the Martins' car, chatting with Beth while her husband John drove them away from the isolated house. Bouncing over the rough road, they waved at others who were then climbing into their cars, and they spoke of the lost couple.

"Where do you think they are," Mary asked, directing her question to her own husband, Ed, who had led a party that had tromped about the woods.

Ed had merely sat, unspeaking for a moment, picking at the beggars lice that clung to his legs, plucking the stubborn seeds from the fabric with old fingers and flinging them like hardened specks of snot out of the car window. He peeled a final seed from his fingers and spoke.

"I don't know, Mary. I don't know where they are. It's the damndest thing, really. All of their stuff is there. Nobody stole nothin' that we can see; and Billy's truck is sittin' there in the yard, with his keys in the house nex` to their bed. An' money in his wallet, too." He squinted, craning his neck a bit to peer back into the cloud of sand raised in the wake of John Martin's car. "I don't think anybody robbed 'em or anything like that."

"Then what," asked Beth, turning to look at her two best friends.

John spoke up. "It's like Ed says, Beth. We just don't know where they could be unless they just wandered off in the woods there and got lost."

"But y'all searched everywhere, didn't you?" Beth's white hair blew in the wash of air that rushed in through lowered windows. She wished she had pulled a scarf over her head as Mary had done.

"We did that," John said, remembering the day of searching, beating the brush for snakes, peering under heavy growth and into thickets that should have been alive with pit vipers. If they had been on a rattlesnake roundup, they would have done poorly. It was strange that they had seen no poisonous snakes, but thank goodness for small blessings. "We busted our buns looking for those two. Believe me, if they had been within a mile in any direction of the farm, we would have found them."

"I don't think they're out there, John. We looked everywhere, and I don't see how..." Ed winced, placing his hand over his mouth as he belched silently. Mary was watching.

"Are you okay, Ed?" She patted his back, noting the dampness of sweaty fabric there, remembering how hot it had been, and reminded of Ed's growing frailty. It was hard to get used to his failing health, for he had always been such a robust man.

"I'm fine. It's just the sandwiches, I reckon. My stomach's just actin' up, is all."

"Here," she said, fumbling about in her purse. "I brought along a pack of Tums in case you got indigestion." She reached in the big handbag, fishing for the plastic bottle. The small foil-wrapped cylinders had proved in recent months not to last the week for Ed, so she had taken to buying the large bottles for him, not knowing that the stuff was merely masking the symptoms of a growing ulcer.

Watching, waiting for the medicine, Ed reached out as Mary withdrew her hand from her purse. But she didn't have the bottle in her fingers.

"What's that, Mary?"

She stared at the oblong section of material, gazing as if mesmerized by it.

Ed, bile rising and burning at his esophagus, stared also at what she held. "Is that someone's key ring?"

Gripping the thing in her spotted fingers, she could not speak. Beth, who still sat turned in the front seat, craned her neck to see, also. "Whose is it," she asked, assuming it was, indeed, the leather handle of someone's key chain.

"I don't know what it is," Mary finally said, answering Ed's question. "And I don't know how it got there," she added, addressing Beth.

"What's that design on it?" Ed reached for the thing, curious of the red markings etched on it.

Before he could touch it, though, Mary had her window rolled completely down. The section of stiff leather sailed out, skimming over the guardrail of the bridge that spanned Fanner's Creek. The last Ed saw of it, the patch was tumbling, changing from dark brown to red as it spun, till he lost sight of it below the rusted metal railing that barely kept cars and trucks from falling into the deep, sluggish waters of the creek.

"Damn, Mary! Now why did you go and do that?" Ed rarely cursed, but the stomach acid was burning at his guts, and he had wanted to see the thing.

Mary sat and stared back toward Fanner's Creek, glad to be headed home. She chafed the palm of her hand against the blue cotton fabric of her dress, trying to clean the filth away.

"What was it, Mary?" John continued along; no one had asked him to stop, and the object was undoubtedly at the bottom of the creek by now.

"I don't know," she said, gazing at her hand as she continued to rub her palm on her dress. "But that writing on it..." She stared, trying to fathom what she had seen, could not piece together the sensations running through her mind and the design that had been drawn there.

"What was it, Mary?" He asked her again. "All I saw was a spot of red. What did it say?" Beth watched Mary's hand: back and forth along her knee. Back and forth, scrubbing.

"It was bad," she said. "There was something bad about it."

Bad could not begin to convey the feeling of complete filth that now flooded over her. Her hand would never be clean. "Who could've put that in my purse," she asked, incredulous.

"Well, I guess we won't know, since you threw it away!" Ed glared at her for a moment, grabbed her purse and found the bottle of antacid for himself. As he chewed a tablet, feeling a bit of relief, he calmed, his little anger fleeing with the arrival of the temporary comfort. Turning to look back at the bridge, he watched as another car followed from the Wishon farm. "I wonder whose it was," he mused, not knowing that Mary had saved the two of them.

In a few minutes, when John and Beth dropped them off at their house, they stood in their yard and waved to the other couple. In Beth's own pocketbook, at the bottom amidst her housewife detritus, where she would not find it, lay a similar object going with them to their home. Ed and Mary waved goodbye to the Martins.

As always, since he'd left his father's home and gone out to make his own life, Ernie Butler spent the evening by himself. He'd never had a wife, had never wanted a family, and since he'd been so independent for so very long, never felt a need for much company.

But tonight had been a different matter, for some reason.

He couldn't quite put his finger on it, but he felt the need for some company, this time. For a while, after leaving the Wishon farm, he had sat in the well-manicured grass behind his house, reclining in his favorite lawn chair, sipping tea and dabbing at the sweat that beaded and dribbled down the surface of his ample belly. He had merely lain, waiting for the sun to set, relaxing after exerting himself in the heat of the day. It was something he was accustomed to doing. He often took down a lawn chair from a hook in the storage room at the rear of the house and unfolded it to while away the lazy hours of summer afternoons. He was accustomed to doing just that, as he pleased, lying and sipping and waiting for the night.

Sitting now in his well-lit den, he thought of the darkness outside and realized that he was frightened. He was frightened of the dark for what must have been the first time in his life. Even as a child, he had never been afraid of shadows, had never thought of unseen things that might lie in wait for a kid with an overactive imagination: things that crouch under beds and in closets when the lights go out, waiting, waiting. Those petty fears had always been for others; not for Ernie Butler.

Until tonight.

With his plump hands rubbing at his cheeks, he recalled how quickly the night had fallen. It was strange. He couldn't remember ever seeing night come on in just such a fashion. Ernie had been leaning back in the chair, feeling the cool trickle of sweet tea on his tongue, and he'd closed his eyes, enjoying the taste. And just that quickly, the twilight had gone to pitch.

For a startled moment, Ernie had thought that he'd fallen asleep for an hour or so. But the glass was still to his lips when he reopened his eyes, and the ice still bobbed in the unseen drink, and his back did not ache as it sometimes did when he fell asleep in that particular lawn chair (he had another one meant for sleeping in). It had just been that the evening had instantly gone from vague sunlight peeking through the pines, to complete darkness painting the forest about his house in tones of tar.

Feeling panicked, he had jumped up from his chair and had stumbled his way to the back door and inside his unlit house.

At the screen, he had paused, wondering about the darkened rooms in there. For the first time in his life, he had actually feared his own house. Still, the pricking at his back was overwhelming and he quickly opened the door, its hinges squeaking wildly; and he had gone in and turned on most of the lights in most of the rooms, not wanting to admit to himself that he was frightened of anything, much less the dark.

After that, the wind had risen. Just as suddenly as the night had fallen, so had the storm begun. It wasn't as if the breeze had slowly picked up, first tickling at tree limbs, then gusting as time passed; the wind had just seemed to smash through the piney barrens around Woodvine, bending trunks, singing a scary tune through green needle lips. It was not, Ernie decided, a right night.

So it was almost no surprise at all when the rain slashed against panes, smacking wetly in great dollops against his windows, crashing down on his secure roof, battering against it with a million little fists. By this time, Ernie was definitely alarmed, and considered actually trying to race over to his nearest neighbors, Ed and Mary Childress. But the rain slashed down at the instant of that idea, washing it away as surely as the water that flowed in his now flooded yard. By the time he could make such a mad dash, he would be soaked to the skin, and Ed and Mary would wonder what he was up to. The idea was foolish, and he knew he had to get hold of himself and stop such thoughts before they turned to panic. He didn't think he had ever panicked in his life, and he didn't want to start now that he was beginning to feel his age.

Perhaps that was it. Perhaps he was merely feeling his age, having to own up to his mortality; maybe those ideas bothered him more than he cared to admit. Maybe...

He had felt that very, very first vibration. Not the second, or the third, or the sixth or seventh as they grew louder, nearer.

The first.

Logically, he wanted to think that it was the storm: perhaps trees were falling over like dominoes in the wind; maybe someone's garage had collapsed under the weight of the slashing rain. Logically, that is what Ernie wanted to think; but he knew what the vague noises were. They were footsteps. They were footsteps and they seemed to be (no, they were!) headed straight for his house.

Ernie knew the lay of the land around his house. He had lived in it for forty years, and he knew every tree and every yard around his own. And he could tell that the steps were thudding directly for his home. There was no doubt about it. Realizing this, he went from room to room, switching off lights, making certain that each window was locked tight against the night.

As he halted before each window, checking for leaks, he peered out into the storm and was rewarded only with glimpses of sheets of black torn out of some pit.

The steps came on, growing closer.

And, there being no explanation for the sounds other than the one he had managed; there being no reasoning at all for the sudden banishment of twilight, for the immediate storm, Ernie's growing fear blossomed into fulsome panic. The steady, intermittent thudding had increased in heartbeat rhythm until whatever was producing it must certainly be only a short distance away.

Then, he could hear it sloshing through the forest, stamping down upon the saturated loam at the edge of his yard, although he could see nothing but night black. It was at that point that Ernie could actually glimpse a shape hovering in air above him: a reddish, twisting sign that seemed to grow and glisten as he watched. It was shaped just as the etching on the portion of dried leather that had been stowed in the pocket of the overalls he had worn to the Wishon farm--the bit of leather he had not found. The thudding halted. The shape spinning over Ernie's head settled down upon him, merging with his fat body sweating fear.

The roof above his head came off, and Ernie Butler screamed, looking up at something huge bearing down on him; he screamed until jaws clamped shut about him, tearing him apart.

A quarter of a mile away, lying in his bed, Ed Childress slept and heard nothing. But he was like that; his wife had often accused him of being able to sleep through an earthquake.

As for his wife, Mary would later wonder if she had heard Ernie's death scream. Actually, she would never be sure, since the storm was raging so, blotting out almost every sound that might compete with itself. Also, she was preoccupied at that particular moment, for she was bandaging her right hand. In the hours since she had touched the thing in the Martin's car, she had managed to rub her palm down to raw flesh.

You could see tendons quite clearly.

Even nearer to the Childress home, John and Beth Martin actually saw what had lumbered up to their house. Despite the storm, they tried to run.
They almost made it to their car.

With the storm, the night dragged on, till daylight broke them both.

CHAPTER EIGHTEEN

In the night, in the worst part of the storm, Davis had made his way to Michelle's house despite the risk. The mere task of struggling to his pickup truck had drenched him from head to toe and through his clothing to his skin. But he had gotten to the truck. The engine had started quickly, and the drive had been slow, the meager headlights doing little save illuminate the driving sheets of white that bashed ceaselessly at his windshield. Still, his memory had served him well, and he drove as much on instinct as by sight to Michelle's house where he had knocked for what seemed a long time until she came to the door. The storm had practically driven him through the opened door, bringing with him buckets of water.

He realized how he must have looked to her.

"Davis!"

At first, he had expected her to ask him what in the hell he was doing there. But...

"Oh, Davis! I was so afraid!" And then she had hugged him in spite of the fact that he was wringing wet and she was getting herself wet, also. "I'm so glad you're here!"

Mr. Hearn's clothes fit him relatively well, Davis found, happy to be dry and not alone this night. He sat with Michelle on the couch in her den, where they had sat on other nights not so awful as this one. Outside, the wind had not abated, and the rain still came down in a near flood. Davis was amazed that the ceiling had sprung no leaks, as yet, and would not be surprised to soon hear water dripping through the roof. They sat in silence, both feeling uneasy, but glad for the company. Davis pulled Michelle closer to him, his blue cotton pajamas slithering over her flannel nightgown. His arms were firm around her; she nestled into his shoulder.

"It hasn't let up a bit," she said to him, her voice barely a whisper over the clatter of rain on everything.

"Nope. I haven't seen one like this since I was a kid."

Actually, Davis had never seen a storm quite like this one, but he didn't want to worry Michelle even more than she was. There was something strange about the storm, about the night. There was something strange in all of what had been happening, but Davis just held it in, seeing no need to bother Michelle. He didn't want anything to bother her, realizing that she had become more important to him than he'd thought. She was more than someone merely to be with. She was someone to protect.

Michelle was someone to love.

Davis bent his head and kissed her lightly on her forehead.

"Do you want to marry me?"

The rain lashed against the house, wanting in. Wind screamed wetly through the pines, like soaking switches slapping soft, exposed flesh. In the cool, blue light of a lone table lamp glowing in the hallway, Michelle nuzzled closer to Davis, feeling secure in his presence, happy to be close to him.

She thought of how afraid she had been when the storm had struck, how worried she had been, wondering how Davis was doing alone in his house with only grouchy old Mr. Gunn as a neighbor. Michelle had been afraid of how Davis was weathering the storm, whether or not his house was secure against the rain. She had worried so, and worrying, realized how much she cared for him, knowing that she loved him when he had appeared at her door.

"Yes, Davis. I want to marry you." She kissed him.

They made love there on the wide couch, in the near darkness.

Through the howl of the storm, they did not hear the visitation brought upon Woodvine. They did not realize what was happening around them. For the remainder of the night, they lived in ignorance, until the sun rose over the pines the next morning.

CHAPTER NINETEEN

In the morning, when the sun came over the trees, breaking through the dark clouds that hovered over them, Addie had gone to her front door.

During the night, her tin roof had barely leaked, (though the rain had drummed angrily against it), and only above her kitchen sink where it did no more harm than the noisy drip of water against stainless steel. Looking out over what had been her yard, she was amazed that the roof had held as well as when Roy had first raised it; for the sandy earth that had stretched out from her porch and into the pines was but a soaking memory.

The land outside her house resembled nothing so much as the swamp that lay at the headwaters of Fanner's Creek, as if the swamp had awakened and stretched its slimy arms, flinging them miles wide.

Something that glistened in the pale light arched liquidly in the shallows near her front porch, and Addie drew back, thinking she had seen eyes in a triangular head staring up at her. She blinked and looked again, but whatever it had been was gone; a ripple spread out from there.

Feeling afraid, she retreated to her kitchen where she went to her refrigerator and drew out a pitcher of water. The contents inside were still cold, for the power had been off only an hour or so before the storm had ceased, as if the tempest had been waiting until the very end to do such a thing. Through the window to her right, she could see where the limb of a big post oak had snapped off and had broken the power line. There must have been another break further away, for the far end of the snapped line merely lay in a sandy puddle. It did not flicker and sputter there.

She returned the pitcher to the box, wishing she had drawn another container or two before the power had gone off. Now her pump would not be operating, and she surely didn't want to risk drinking from the creek after such a storm as the night before. At any rate, she was too afraid for now to even try walking (or wading!) down to the creek.

There was something weird about the outside, just now, as if she had seen something at the door, but hadn't realized it at the time. Rising, glass in hand, she went back to her door and peered out. Seeing, she almost dropped the glass.

Above the line of green pines that circled about her little house, she could see something that had not been there before the storm. Past the first stand of evergreens, something jutted above them, lifting above their twenty year old crowns. It was another tree; one that had not been there only hours before, great yellow fronds drooping, light glimmering as from a waxed surface. Again, Addie retreated to her kitchen, this time pulling the front door closed behind her.

Something stirred in the water outside. She heard it splash, once, then small ripples tapped against the bricks upon which her front porch rested.

Addie thought about Rick from the church: his young face bright with smiles, asking her if she wouldn't like to come back to town with him. Oh, she would, she would today, if only he were here. Peering out of the kitchen window, she could see another of the trees and knew that they had not been washed, somehow, down the flooded banks of Fanner's Creek to those points at which they now stood. And she was afraid that Rick would not be coming to see her today. She was afraid that no one from the church would be making the journey out to her isolated little house.

Far away, from the direction of Thirty Acre Rock, Addie heard something like the growl of a big motorboat hissing out over the sticky wind. It was not, she knew, a motorboat. And for their sakes, she dearly hoped that no one from the church would try to make it out to her house today.

Something had gone wrong. Red didn't know what had happened, but nothing like it had ever occurred in all the times he had performed the ritual. And it wasn't merely the storm that had lashed the town; there was something else, something he did not understand, and did not know how to control. There was something wrong with the countryside about the town, around the Rock.

Strange, twisted trees stood in places where before there had only been pines and oaks. The waters of Fanner's Creek had seemed to creep higher, and were darker than they should have been. Even the air seemed cut with a strange clarity--almost stingingly clear. In the moist earth he had seen tracks that had not been made by anything he had ever seen, and something gray, with smooth skin, had peered up at him from the tea colored water of the rampant Fanner's Creek; it had vanished before he could tell what it might be. Almost, Sage was frightened.

At the moment, he had to send back the thing he had called, as he always did after it had completed its tasks. He could only assume that the ritual would work, again, as it always had. But he couldn't know that, for he was not so different from a child who knew how to operate an auto, yet had no inkling of what made it work, the forces that drive the engine.

Actually, Red thought, his knowledge was less even than that, for he couldn't truly admit that he could even steer his awful machine. He only knew how to turn the key.

Standing upon the pocked surface of the Rock, the old man had to etch again the mark he must make. The paint took on the terrible dimensions upon the stone beneath his guiding hand. His mind twisted the figure, opening the way, unlocking doors, removing barriers that would fall again on passing. In the feeble light of morning, he uttered the sounds that returned the order of things. Above him, in the glittering air, shapes took form, dancing, thrown out by the strange equation that twisted from forgotten corridors in his mind.

From far away, he felt the thunder of the thing's tread, stamping the rain wet earth beneath it. As it approached, he could feel its anger, realizing that it was once again to be pressed back into that place that was not life. Red wondered, sometimes, why it did not try to stop him, why it always went slavishly back to where it had come. But it always did.

Sooner than he had expected, it burst from the cover of the trees, glistening magnificently in the feeble light of the rising sun. Dark clouds straggled overhead, alternately blocking and releasing the bright rays. The beast stood, armored, colored in reptilian yellows, striped in orange that glazed its scaled length. Great nostrils twitched, breathing in the essence of the little thing that danced and capered at its taloned feet, seeing in it something akin to the meat that gored the fat muscles that worked its jaws, not quite recognizing in Sage the blood that had poured in rivers from its teeth, that painted its throat. It wanted to resist the force that was calling to it, that would soon press it back into that dark place that was not a place. But it could not resist. Still...

As Red completed his task, he opened wide squinting eyes and saw as the way was opened, as the thing was drawn back, winking out of existence. And as it began to fade, he watched and heard the great jaws creak wide, a call as of ten thousand eagles screaming into the wind.

Then it was gone; Red was alone on the pitted stone.

And he could not be certain that he hadn't heard something return that call from somewhere not terribly far away.

CHAPTER TWENTY

"What happened?" She asked him, looking out in the bright sun shining through air that fairly stung their noses with its metallic scent--air cut as clean as any they'd ever smell.

"I don't know." Down the way, toward the square, Davis could see limbs across the road, bits of green and splintered wood torn from trunks gleaming pale yellow in the morning light. Beyond that there was a spill of lumber from what had been someone's yard. He stepped from Michelle's porch, making his way through slowly receding puddles that lazily steamed. The ground squelched in the still air.

"Where are you going, Davis?" Michelle clenched her hands about the blue housecoat, tugging it tightly about her small shoulders. She didn't ask him not to leave her, but he could hear the implication in her voice.

Looking back, seeing her standing frightened in the doorway, Davis did not want to leave her alone. But he also did not want to take her with him, not knowing what he might find in the storm ravaged community. "I'm just going to walk down the road a bit and see what's happening. I won't go far and I won't be gone for long."

"I want to come with you. Let me to get dressed." She waited for him to come back up.

"No, Michelle. I don't want you coming with me until I see what's happening around here. I don't see anyone else on the street, the phones are dead--at least yours is--and I can't imagine why someone from Martinsville hasn't come over to see how we're doing after such a storm." He looked away, gazing down the road, his eyes scanning for movement.

"It must have been a twister," he told her. "I've never seen one, but I reckon that must be what hit us. And if it was a twister, surely there should be someone to come out and check up on Woodvine." He rubbed a hand across his unshaved face. "I mean, we may not be much, but we're people. And we're out here and they need to send someone to check up on us, Goddamn it!"

"Davis. I'm afraid." Michelle remained in the doorway, watching Davis with frightened eyes. If he left her, she would be alone, no one left to take up for her, and no one left to look after her. No one. And the idea scared her more than she had ever suspected it would. Davis Ryan was the last person left in Woodvine who seemed to care about the rest of the people there. If anything happened to him, all of those remaining would be more alone than any of them suspected.

"I have to check up on some people, Michelle. You just stay put, don't go anywhere, and I'll be back as quick as I can." He took a few steps, turned and looked questioningly to her. "Can you do that for me?"

"Yes." She knew he had to look. "I'll wait here and I won't leave."

"Good." He made as if to go, then turned again to her. "And lock the door. Okay?"

"Okay." She closed it and he waited until he heard the deadbolt drive home.

What was going on?

Slowly, Davis made his way down the once familiar road, feeling gravel beneath his boots. The hardtop had been poured back in '59, and it was nearly solid black from uncounted patches poured during the intervening years. And there were dozens of slowly widening potholes that had yet to be patched, that should have been repaired long ago. Vapor rose in slow, tenuous ropes from the small pools that lay in the pockmarked roadbed. Almost as slowly, Davis moved along the street.

Walking through the neighborhood, Davis could see that most of the homes were intact, had survived the storm with no outward damage beyond a few torn shingles, the odd gutter hanging from battered eaves. There were no roofs torn from frames, and he saw not a single body lying in the non-existent ruins he had expected to find.

The tumble of wood he had seen from Michelle's yard turned out to be what was left of the Martin couple's carport. The clapboard walls and tin roof were broken down and strewn from yard to street, scattered like the toys of some petulant toddler. The car still sat in its formerly sheltered spot, sound except for a few dents and dings Davis could not be sure weren't there before the storm. Looking toward the house, he could see that the front door stood open.

He pressed on, meaning to go past, to the home of their friends, Ed and Mary Childress.

Their front door stood open.

He stopped, his boots making a loud scuffing sound atop uneven gravel set in asphalt. The old man stared at the door, watching as water dripped slowly from above, making little patting noises at the base of the threshold. Even from where he stood, he could see that rain had streamed into the house. Beyond the door, water glistened in the foyer of the Childress home. And Davis Ryan knew full well that Mary Childress never allowed a mess in her house. Not when she had raised three boys (Ed had once complained to him that was the reason their boys rarely came to visit with their own families), not since those boys had grown and left home, and certainly not in the recent visits Davis had made to the Childress household.

After standing, staring at the doorway propped partially open, tempting him to come up, Davis did just that. He hopped across the water-filled ditch that separated the yard from the road, lighting in the spongy lawn and sending a spray of moisture spreading out. And still the morning was as quiet as the slight breeze that failed to stir water-heavy limbs dangling from the trees that had survived the night. With some trepidation, he moved up the walkway to the front door. Feeling the need, but fearing there really was none, he knocked. "Ed? Mary?" There was no answer, of course.

Waiting politely for the reply he knew was not forthcoming, Ryan stepped into the house. The carpet in the foyer squished wetly, and he was aware that the door had been open for most of the night, for almost the entire storm, probably. The wallpaper on the nearest walls was full of bubbles that had formed beneath it, and the corners of the stuff were stubbornly peeling from pasted moorings along the wall. Water soaked everything. The small cherry table that had stood by the door, decorated by baskets of dried wildflowers, was broken into once dry bits on the floor. Past that, he could see a thin sheen of water lying over most surfaces.

The inside of the house was thick with humidity, and very quiet.

"They ain't here."

The voice that came from within the house startled Davis. He jumped as the sound came out of the darkness within, and it took him a second to recognize it as that of Ed Childress.

"God, Ed! You damned near scared the Hell out of me!"

From out of the shadows, the other man walked over, moving slowly. "They ain't here."

"Where are they? Why would they let the storm into their home like this?"

Childress sighed heavily, and in the gloom, Davis could see his right hand dart to his mouth, watched as he chewed another antacid tablet. "I honestly don't know, Davis. I can't imagine Beth lettin' this happen to her house."

"How long have you been here?" Davis went further in. He put his fingers to an oil painting hanging on the wall.

"Not more than ten minutes. Been tryin' to look around and see if I can figure out where they went."

"Their car's still here."

"Yeah. But John always keeps his car keys hangin' on a hook in the kitchen, an' they ain't there. He must've taken 'em down when they tried to get out of here." Ed absently toed at a linen napkin lying soaked on the floor.

"Tried to get out? Did they tell you they were trying to get out? Did you phone him last night?"

Childress moved on over to where Davis was standing. The younger man could hear as Ed crunched chalky stuff between his molars. "No." Ryan could see pale white coating Ed's tongue as he spoke. "It's Mary. Says she heard something last night."

"What?"

There was an awkward silence as Ed turned it over and over in his mind. His wife was sleeping now, her hand securely bandaged as she dozed in a drugged stupor; full of Valium. He debated telling Davis what Mary had said to him. "Some kind of noise, Davis. Just some kind of noise."

"Well? What kind of noise? Tell me! A motor? Wind? What?"

Stupid. Crazy. And he'd slept through it all. "It don't make sense, Davis. She was just havin' a nightmare is all."

Ryan grasped Childress by the shoulder, squeezing with fingers that were still quite strong. "Don't give me that! I don't care if it doesn't make sense! The Wishons disappearin' doesn't make sense, either! Now, what did she hear?"

"She said she heard footsteps!"

"Footsteps?" Davis almost whispered it? "In your house?"

"No. Not in the house. Outside. In the woods."

"What kind of footsteps could she have heard outside in that storm?"

"Giant ones." Ed would have laughed if someone else had said it, if he hadn't been standing in John and Beth's rain soaked home.

"Shit!" Davis' hand was off of Ed's shoulder and he was moving quickly through the Martin house toward the back door. The floors were not wet toward the rear rooms and his boots clumped on dry wood rather than splashed in puddles. In the kitchen, he unlatched the deadbolt and went out on the small porch beyond so that he could look into the piney woods that bordered their yard as it did all the yards of Woodvine.

"What are you lookin' for?" Ed was with him, and Davis absently noted that the older man was massaging his shoulder.

Davis peered at the green forest. Sunlight glittered in uncounted droplets hanging from thick needles, making prism points everywhere he looked. Many of the trees bore broken limbs that lay far from where they had grown. Some trees had even been pushed over, snapped at the trunk.

"What do you see?" It was Ed again.

Behind the house, almost in the center of the lawn, the neat rows of planted pines seemed to have been shunted aside, as the rows of corn in Billy Wishon's field had been shunted aside. But he couldn't be certain. The wind could very well have blown them apart in such a manner. "I ain't sure, Ed." He went down the concrete stairs to the soaking yard, and further, toward the waiting trees. His heart beat heavily. He was genuinely afraid.

"Come with me," he told Ed.

The two of them went to the pines, walking past the well-mowed lawn the Martins kept so neat. They went on past it and into the verge of the pulpwood forest. Davis scanned the forest floor, looking down on the surface all rusty with years-old pine straw, dotted here and there with palmetto, bear grass, and bramble thickets. There were no tracks in the thick matting. And if there had been, then the storm would certainly have washed them away.

He sighed, placed his hands on his hips, and threw his head back.

And saw.

"Shit."

"What is it, Davis?"

Ryan went over to the nearest tree. Halfway up its thirty foot height the bark had been rubbed off in a two foot strip on one side. The tree adjacent to it was similarly marked. As were the two trees in the row behind it. And the ones behind those. And so on. He pointed up at the uniform blemishes that mirrored off and off into the forest, lost in the green. "Do you see it?"

"What did that, Davis? Not the wind."

He looked into Ed's face. "No. Not the wind."

"Then what did it? A backhoe? Why would someone drive a backhoe through the woods in the middle of a storm?" Childress stared into the woods with an expression that bordered on hysteria. No one drove a backhoe through the pines to John's house, and he didn't want to think of impossibilities. He was ready to ask again, but he turned to see Davis trotting swiftly across the soaked yard, boots sending up spray as he went.

"Where are you going?"

Davis didn't answer.

CHAPTER TWENTY-ONE

Red Sage had slept through the morning. He would've liked to have been able to say that he had slept well through it, that nothing had disturbed him at all and that he had dozed quietly contented while the town had awakened to find what had happened in the night. But Sage had not slept soundly. Oh, he had slept, although the hours had been marked by restlessness, and something like nightmares. He was surprised that he could still have a nightmare; Sage had thought that he was far beyond such things.

Something had bothered him as he tossed and turned in his bed. Something had not so much frightened him, as bothered him. He was worried that something would stop him; that something would ruin all of his well laid plans and prevent him from wresting greatness from the entropy that was slowly killing Woodvine. He couldn't abide that. He couldn't die without having accomplished what he had set out to do.

And he knew where the threat lay. It was Addie Lacher, that black woman who lived out past the farthest farmhouse, out where Piney Grove Road tailed out into logging tracks and a pair of sandy ruts. He'd not been there in more than thirty years, but he knew where she was. He figured the last families had moved out at the end of the sixties, out with everyone else who had eased on over to Martinsville or to Macon and Thomasville and even Atlanta.

They were all gone or going, the blacks with the whites. Red would have admired the old woman for her sheet tenacity and stubbornness if he didn't currently hate her so much. She'd have to go before she could possibly do something to ruin what remained of his plans. He doubted she could do anything on her own, but Davis Ryan was sticking his nose in where it might do the most harm, and he couldn't deal with more than one threat at the moment. There was the worry, too, that Ryan might go for outside help as he had already down, and Sage could only hope that the bastard had not made it through the night.

There was the added concern that after the storm, the people of Martinsville might come poking about to make certain that nothing was amiss. In fact, he could most assuredly expect such a thing to happen after the severity of the winds and rain that had lashed Woodvine during the night. It had seemed to have been localized, so he still held onto the slim hope that the sheriff in their county seat would not bother to see how the forgotten community was making out.

Still, he also knew that the storm had been the result of what he had been doing, that his repeated calling of the beast was disrupting other forces. You couldn't do such a thing as often as he had and not expect some unknown reaction. Sage wasn't worried about that, for he was almost finished. They were all nearly done.

In the meantime, he would have to make certain that no one remained to stop him. Davis Ryan had to go, and quickly; and the Lacher woman would have to be taken care of. He would finish off

Ryan, but he didn't have the time to go chasing through the woods for an old nigger woman; he knew someone quite more suited to that, someone who would even enjoy it. He rose up from crisp sheets, standing stiffly and strode over to his dresser where he opened a trio of drawers and began to draw out fresh clothes.

He'd personally take care of Ryan, but first he would pay a quick visit to see Mark Kiser. Kiser, in turn, would pay an overdue visit to Addie Lacher. Red would see to it.

In the end, Sage hadn't had to mince words with Mark. He had actually come right out and said it: "Mark, I want you to ride out Piney Grove Road and kill the old nigra woman who lives over there." In spite of everything, in spite of the town coming to the end of its life (as far as Kiser knew), and in spite of he being an old man nearing the end of his own life, Kiser had been almost shocked to hear the words coming out of Red's mouth. It wasn't that Mark thought that Sage gave a damned about the black woman, or about any black; it was just the matter-of-factness of it all.

He just never thought the old liar would come right out and say anything he meant without walking circles around the point and leaving it up to others to figure out what he really meant.

Kiser hadn't answered the former mayor for several seconds.

He had merely stared back at the other man, staring hard into Red's chiseled face, saying nothing. And then.

"Red, you know I never questioned nothin' you ever told me to do. Not ever. You've told me to do a lot of shady shit in our day, an' I never asked you nothin'. I just did what you asked me to do. An' mostly it was good for both of us, an' good for things in general."

"Mark..."

"No. Wait. I ain't sayin' I won't do it. But I just want to know what's goin' on. That's all." Kiser remained where he was seated at his kitchen table, sipping the hot coffee in the mug before him. Now, for the first time in his life, he actually felt as if he were on an equal footing with Red Sage; for the first time, he knew that he had something Sage needed and that there was nowhere else for the old schemer to go.

"What do you want to know? Do you want to know why I want her dead? Is that it?" Sage continued to stand. He felt more comfortable standing, looking down on the brute who had been his to control in better days, and his to control still.

"I cain't really say that I give a damn why you want me to scratch that old woman. I don't give a damn, at all. But I can see out my window. I can look down the road an' see the Childress home, an' I stood on my front porch an' listened to people talkin' back an' forth to each other. There's others missin' this mornin'.

"Just like them Wishons. An' I know that you know exactly what's happenin' in this town. I want to know, too." Kiser lifted the mug and slurped at the steaming coffee, his eyes drilling a hole in Red's own hard gaze.

Sage knew that Kiser would kill the woman for him. He knew it as certainly as he knew how to breathe. But he couldn't have the former police chief dallying, quizzing him on things that no longer mattered. He had things to do, and he had to do them quickly with no one to threaten him. But he also knew that even Kiser might balk if he knew what was truly happening.

"Mark?"

"Yeah?"

"You remember Woodvine. You remember what we used to be when the mills were working and the schools were full and people came here to build homes and open businesses, when people lived here!"

"Yeah, I remember. But I ain't in the mood for a speech, Red. I just want to know what in Hell's name is going on." He breathed, took another slug of coffee.

"Woodvine's all but dead, Mark. You know that. I just don't want the town to die like this. And it won't, if you'll just help me." He stared back at his crony, wanting to be gone, wanting Kiser to be on his way into the woods to kill Addie Lacher so that he could, himself, finish off the remainder of his opposition, as he had finished off everyone who had ever gotten too much in his way.

"You ain't go'n' tell me, are you?" Kiser set his cup down and slowly shook his head from side to side, chuckling to himself.

"All I'm saying is that I always wanted good things for Woodvine, and that I want something great for it now, before it's too late for something great. Do you see?"

Kiser stood up, drawing himself nearly as straight and almost as tall as Red was. He smiled at Red, cleared his throat and strode across the kitchen to where his .357 was lying cleaned and loaded on the cabinet top, green linoleum below it, brown stained cabinets overhanging it.

"Fuck it, Red. I guess it don't really matter whether I know what's goin' on, or not. Reckon I'll find out soon enough." He cleared his throat again and fingered the newly oiled barrel. "She's good as dead. Hell, it was worth it just to hear you come out and ask something plain as day, for once." He laughed.

Behind him, he could hear Sage turn and march crisply to the door, the hinges on the screen whine scratchily. "Thanks, Mark. You're doing all of Woodvine a great favor."

As Sage's hard soles clacked on wooden steps, Kiser called out.

"Red! I will find out what's goin' on, won't I?"

"Oh, yes! I can promise you that, my friend!" And while Kiser went about his house gathering on his clothes and preparing himself, Red Sage paused at the old chief's car and left him a small gift of leather and of paint which he placed beneath the seat where Kiser would never see it.

CHAPTER TWENTY-TWO

Davis didn't like to agonize long over a problem. He worked best when he could see what was wrong, figure his most logical course of action (he never second-guessed himself), and then he did it. It was a simple way to tackle obstacles; it had worked most of his life, more often than not. And so he had not wanted to worry about particulars when he knew that what must be done was to get over to Martinsville and get some help.

Michelle's phone was dead, and so was Ed's. He didn't bother to go running about Woodvine searching in vain for a phone that was operating. The fastest way to expedite matters was to drive to Martinsville as quickly as possible.

Mary Childress was more asleep than awake, more delirious than calm and Ed refused to leave her alone. But Davis needed someone with him to back up his story and Ed's car was faster than his truck, so he put Michelle in care of Mary. He refused to take a *No* from Ed. They were going, and they were going together, and Ed was going to give Davis the keys so that they could leave. Right now. End of discussion.

That was how they found the Georgia Power Company truck.

Davis and Ed stood on what had been the Woodvine side of the bridge across Fanner's Creek. The creek was high, well over its banks and threatening to flood as high as the roadbed on which the two were standing. Thebridge itself was broken, sheared off a half dozen feet from the tips of Davis' boots, the far side bent downward so that you could see the twisted and rusty metal arcing down into the tea colored water. Beneath the surface of the creek, they could see that a large truck was submerged there, still on what had been the bridge, its hood pointed toward the sky. It had obviously been headed back toward Martinsville. They could make out the headlights, the Georgia Power logo on the front of the hood, and then the windshield was faded to murky brown the color of dark tea.

"Must've been headed back out," Ed muttered.

"Yeah, he was. I noticed his tire tracks down the way to the Wishon place. Just didn't mention it. He probably went down real early this morning to check up on the substation down there." He went to one knee and tried to peer into the dark, swiftly flowing water.

"You think he got out?"

"I don't know. I can't see well enough through that water to tell if somebody's in the front seat. Damn!" Davis went toward the left side of the bridge abutment, grasping what remained of a support, feeling the rust flake off beneath his rough hand. His boots squished in the wet ground near the water's edge. Again, he went down on one knee, trying to peer through the depths of Fanner's Creek.

"Davis, you be careful! The current's real swift today. If you fell in, you'd get swept away in a second!"

Ed was telling the truth; Davis could barely hear the other man over the constant slosh and gurgle of the swollen creek.

"Yeah, well, I just want to see if that poor guy is still in the cab of that truck. If he isn't, then maybe he's around somewhere. Downstream, or something." Davis squatted, leaning forward so that he could try to see what was in the front seat of the truck. 'Damn! It was frustrating!' He could almost, but not quite, see what was down there.

Straining to peer into the gloomy depths of Fanner's Creek, most sound masked by the flow of the water, Davis never heard the arrival of Red Sage, never heard the tires of the old squad car crunching down on the pocked road, and never heard the snap of twigs under Red's big feet.

But he did feel Red's heel smash into the back of his head.

And he was totally surprised to find himself floundering in the current of Fanner's Creek at full flood. He gasped once, went beneath the surface, his arms flailing as he tried to figure out what was happening. His left boot scraped against the hood of the submerged truck as the water swept him past the bridge and beyond. In seconds, he was gone.

"Red! My God, what have you done? Are you crazy?" Ed stood in front of Red as the other man pulled himself up the bank, bracing himself on the very support Davis had used to climb down. As Red brought himself level, he stood straight, towering over Childress, making him feel smaller than he really was.

Red took a quick look downstream, making certain that Davis Ryan was not pulling himself out of the creek a short distance away, making sure that the current had not deposited him ashore nearby. Childress, too, unlocked his neck long enough to stare in the same general direction for the same reason.

"You should be happy, Ed. You should thank me." Sage picked absently at a bit of dead vegetation that had adhered to his pants leg.

"You killed him, Red! You killed Davis Ryan." Ed moved toward the edge of the creek, but Sage had his big hand on the smaller man's shoulder before he could take more than a single step. Hard fingers dug painfully into Childress' flesh.

"If I hadn't done something, there's no telling what he might've done. More than likely, Mary would never have seen your face again. As I said, you should thank me, Ed Childress." He did not lessen his grip on Ed's shoulder.

Slowly, Ed relaxed, his posture drooping, his knees almost buckling beneath the pressure of Sage's grip. In response, Sage let up a bit. "Why did you do that? Why?" His voice was no longer high, no longer near hysteria.

"Ed, who do you think has been behind what's been going on? Hm?"

"I don't know what you're talking about, Red."

Sage didn't have to go to this much trouble. He really didn't. All he really had to do was toss this bothersome little man right in after the other bothersome little man. He considered it, but decided not to. "Davis Ryan was going to do the same thing to you that he did to Bill and Shelley Wishon. The same thing that he did to John and Beth Martin."

"What do you mean, Red?" Sage's claw like fingers were off of his shoulder, now; reward for his exhibition of calm.

"He killed them, Edward. Davis Ryan killed those poor souls just as certainly as he's now at the bottom of Fanner's Creek. I knew he did it, and if I hadn't taken care of him just now, then I know that you wouldn't have come back with him from your little ride."

Childress remained where he was, shaking his head, muttering. "No, Red. You're wrong. Davis didn't do anything. You shouldn't have, Red. You shouldn't..."

"Shut up! Shut up and get yourself back home!" He leaned into the command, and Ed thought that he was surely going to strike him. "Well? I'm waiting! Get in your car and get the hell back home!"

"I...I can't, Red. My keys." And he pointed toward Fanner's Creek.

Sage would have laughed, but it wouldn't have looked good.

So he merely pushed Ed toward the old squad car and made him get inside. He climbed in after his passenger was seated, and they drove off.

Until it was out of sight, he kept Fanner's Creek in his rear view mirror, watching it all the while. Perhaps he should have waited a little longer, to make sure that Ryan was truly drowned, but he wasn't terribly worried--after all, Davis was an old man.

Wordlessly, Red paused long enough at the Childress driveway so that his passenger could climb out. After that, he waited only long enough for the door to be shut and he was gone. His only worry was that he had not had the opportunity to leave one of his patches with Ed. He thought that if he had merely given the fool one of them, then the man would have been frightened enough to merely take it with no questions asked.

Hell, if he had told Childress to stuff it down his throat the little mouse would probably have done that, too. But, no. He'd do what had to be done later, and not worry about the particulars. If things were going smoothly for Kiser, then the black woman was gone, now, and there was nothing left to stop Sage from doing what he wanted to do.

Nothing at all.

CHAPTER TWENTY-THREE

"Pat! Oh, God, Pat!" Michelle slammed her small fist against the door again and again, until the thick of it began to swell and her knuckles were scraped; she left little spots of blood on the white paint there before Pat could get to the front of his house.

By the time Wilson had his front door open, his pants zipped and his belt buckled, he had begun to hear some of what Michelle was screaming.

Pulling the door open, he barely caught Michelle in his arms as she collapsed into them. He was unshaved, wearing only his pants and an undershirt, his bare feet sticking out of his trousers. Surprised though he was, he kept Michelle from completely falling and helped her to the sofa in his front room.

"Michelle! What are you saying? What's going on?" Through the haze of waking and through the muffling barrier of his house, he had made out just some of what the woman had been screaming at him. Something about Red Sage and Davis.

"It's Davis!" Her eyes were wide and staring, and he could tell that she was on the verge of total panic, shock, perhaps.

"What about him? What's happened to Davis?" He was not a little upset himself, and cursed the beer he had drunk all night long. But the storm had frightened him; actually frightened him and he had found sleep only after making himself royally drunk.

"Now slow down and tell me what's happened. I can't make any sense of what you're sayin' and I cain't help Davis if I don't know what's goin' on. Now calm down and tell me what you know." He knelt in front of her and tried to sound as reasonable as he was able.

She seemed to hear what he was saying. After a moment,

Michelle took a breath and did her best to compose herself. At last, "Ed. Ed Childress and Davis went to go into Martinsville to get some help because John and Beth Martin are missing."

"Missing?"

"Listen to me!" Michelle's anger flared. "You're Davis' best friend! So you listen to me, damn it!" He did.

"They took Ed's car since Davis figured it'd be faster and he needed someone to help him talk some sense into that sheriff over there. But Ed says that the bridge over the spur is out--a Georgia Power truck went over it or something...I don't know, exactly.

"Anyway, Davis and Ed got out to see if someone was still in the truck. If they needed help, you know?" She was edging toward hysteria again. Pat reached out and patted her shoulder.

"I'm listening to you, Michelle. Just take your time and tell me what happened."

"Yes. Yes." She sucked in, sighed. "Well, Davis went down to the edge of Fanner's Creek. And Ed said that the creek is way up, Pat, almost over its banks, almost up to the road. He went down there and Red Sage drove up, only Davis didn't notice and Ed didn't think anything he thought that Red was just going to walk down to the creek to see if he could help too and Davis didn't hear him or see him come up and he...he...he..." The word turned into a gasp, nearly became maniacal laughter. Pat took Michelle in his arms and held her, patting her back.

"It's alright, Michelle. No one can hurt you here. Okay? Now just calm down, catch your breath and tell me what happened. Can you do that?" He continued to stroke her back and began to rock gently, trying to soothe her. *What had happened to Davis? What in Hell's name was that crazy Sage up to?*

There was a moment of silence as Michelle regained her composure. The two merely sat as she began to breathe more easily, trying to set her thoughts so that she would make some sense when she spoke. "What happened next," he asked her, not really wanting to.

"Red Sage went down to where Davis was looking into the creek and he kicked him in the head, Pat! Ed told me that Red just kicked Davis in the back of the head as hard as he could! Then Davis fell into the creek!" Her eyes were full of tears, then, and she was crying, crying. "He didn't come back out, Pat! Ed told me that Davis didn't come back out!

"Can't you do something? Do something, Pat! Do something!"

She was screaming, and Pat didn't know what to do.

As Michelle was hysterically recounting what had happened,

Red was making one final circuit around Woodvine. He couldn't be absolutely certain, but he was pretty sure (damned sure) that he had marked every single house remaining in the community. Every one.

After the storm, after the buzz of what some of them were hearing passing from neighbor to neighbor, no one was terribly surprised to see Red acting in such a strange manner. Wilbur

Jackson was curious enough so that he reached under his front porch to see what Red had tossed down there, and found the bit of leather with the weird little word painted on it; he ended up putting it with a stack of paper on his wife's dresser with the intention of showing it to the sheriff when the lousy bastard finally got into town. No one else bothered to see what he was about. Most of them were frightened of what he might actually do to them. They'd heard about Davis, by then.

And after that, in the full light of day, Red Sage drove the aging squad car, the last official vestige of the town of Woodvine, out to the road that led down to Thirty Acre Rock. And there he worked his magic for what he hoped would be the last time.

CHAPTER TWENTY-FOUR

Something made Addie overcome the terrible fear she was feeling. One of her dreams made her get up, made her have the courage to leave her little house and help someone.

She had been sitting in her favorite chair, merely sitting and nothing more, trying not to think of Fanner's Swamp stretching its fingers out to reach to her front door, trying not to think of the terrible lizard she had seen in her dreams, trying not to recall the thing that had shown its head for an awful moment before darting beneath the water beyond her porch. Sitting there, she had dozed, and when she had begun to sleep, the little brown man with the hole in his chest had come back to visit her.

Addie opened her eyes. Standing before her, much the same as he had been the first time he had appeared to her, was the dead man. His white shirt still had the stain of blood where the bullet had entered his body. He motioned to her and wordlessly he began to speak.

Where before she had actually heard him talking, had heard his strange accent with her own ears, this time she did not specifically hear him. His lips, like the rest of him, were more tenuous than before; she could barely make out his form there in the darkness of her bedroom. But his words were speaking inside her head, speaking as he moved his phantom lips.

Someone needed help, and she was the only one who could give it. The dead man showed her where to go, what to do. Slowly, she got up from her chair, and she went to do what was expected of her. The gift that enabled her to see such things was from God, and she could do no less if He so commanded her. As she went from the house, the dead man walked before her, fading more and more with each step they took. She could see the gaping wound the bullet had made when it had exited his poor body. By the time she made the last stair from her porch, the dead man was all but gone. By the time she began to wind her way down the sodden pathway that led down to Fanner's Swamp, he was gone. Completely.

Walking carefully, but as quickly as her old legs would carry her, she moved away from her little house and into the pines that soon gave way to the cypress trees that marked the edge of the swamp.

And that was why she was away from the house when Kiser came to call.

When Davis had fallen into Fanner's Creek, the current had swept him away from the bank so swiftly that he had not had the chance to grasp any bit of brush or limb that overhung the water.

Struggling against the force of the flood, he had come close to the surface as the bridge moved over his head, and opening his eyes he had caught a quick, fleeting glimpse of what had caused him to pitch forward into the creek. It took all of his will not to curse Red Sage and thereby lose the one gulp of air he had taken when the other man's heel had smashed against the back of his skull. After that, the current was sucking at him again, pulling at his thick boots and doing its best to take him to the bottom of the creek.

By the time Davis' flailing arms had succeeded in taking him close to the surface, he was better than a hundred feet from where the bridge had crossed Fanner's Creek. When he had finally been able to kick the soaked boots free of his feet so that he could force his head out of the water, he was fifty feet further downstream and around the bend that forced the creek southward and then down to Fanner's Swamp. That was why Sage never saw Ryan's pale head break the surface of the creek, and he never heard the single gasp of air that Davis sucked in before the creek took him down again.

Now that Davis was quit of the sodden weight of his work boots, he could kick effectively with his legs and his stroking arms were no longer flailing ineffectively so that he went nowhere. Davis could maneuver himself enough so that he could surface from time to time and take enough of a breath to keep from drowning. And now that he could move himself about, he was able to avoid the half sunken logs that tried again and again to smash into him. But the sections of downed trees flew so swiftly by that he was unable to grasp hold of one so that he could rest or cling to it until it came to rest on one bank or another. He continued to stroke, to kick, and he was glad that he had always been a strong swimmer. With some luck, he thought that he might survive the experience.

The surging water took him closer and closer to Fanner's Swamp. Davis was too busy trying to stay alive to notice that the trees that loomed over him were not trees he had ever seen growing in this or any other place. He was too busy sucking in an occasional breath of wet air to see that Fanner's Swamp had become something it had never been. The man certainly did not notice when something long and sleek noticed him, and noticing him slid smoothly from where it sat perched on a ferny bank and began to pursue his retreating form, slicing easily through water that dragged at Davis and against which he could only thrash and struggle. As Davis splashed, it cut through the dark water, aiming its muzzle toward the bit of warmth it detected in the current ahead. Great teeth waited.

Mark Kiser had had to park his truck a good mile and a half farther from the old woman's house than he had intended. Well, that was okay with him--he'd enjoy the walk and take the extra time to think about it before he blew her head off. After that, he could search through her house and see if there was something worth stealing there, although he doubted there would be. Still, you never could tell, and it would look good for the county cops when they came to snoop around. Hell, they'd think that some young nigger had known about her and had killed her for whatever she had. It made no difference to him whether she really had anything worth taking. He'd enjoy it whether it paid or not.

At the edge of the clearing where her house was located, Kiser left the trail and faded into the woods. It wasn't so much that he was afraid to be seen as the fact that the trail was more flooded than the surrounding forest, and he didn't like the idea of wading through knee deep water to get to her place. It took him a little longer, but he made a half circuit around the plot and cut back toward the house, feeling wet sand squelch beneath his heavy tread as he went. About sixty feet from her house, he came out of the trees so that there was no hiding for him. It was a walk right up and do it kind of job. So that is what he did.

As he got close to the porch, he could see that the front door was standing wide. "Hey!" What the hell. "Hey!" What was her name? He couldn't quite recall. "Lockey! Miz Lockey! It's Officer Kiser! You know, from Woodvine!" Stupid nigger ought to remember him. He'd beaten the shit out of enough of them back when you could get away with that kind of thing. He was almost to the edge of her porch.

"Are you here?" There were little footprints leading away from her door. None leading back.

"Shit." She had gone into the woods, for some reason, although Kiser was damned if he could figure out why. Oh well, he reasoned, it didn't matter where she was, and maybe this would work out for the best: he could kill her there and toss her body in the swamp for the alligators. Hm. Not a bad idea. Just like that little foreign nigger Red Sage had killed way back when. He knew Red had killed the little man, even though Sage had never mentioned it and Kiser had never asked. Strange situation, that.

Sage had taken an interest in him after Kiser had arrested him; he had seen Sage come into the jailhouse and talk to the brown man all night long for two nights. And then he had come in the third night, told Kiser that he wanted the man out, that he was taking him out of town. But Kiser knew better. He had followed Red's car down to the road to Thirty Acre Rock, and he had stayed there until he'd heard the gunshot.

On the far side of the clearing, Kiser followed the tracks that led down a sandy path now more mud than sand. He didn't care; just made her easier to follow. He thought again of the little brown man, the way Sage had acted after meeting him. Strange. Kiser had not thought of that for years and years. Funny the ideas that could hit a man at the oddest times.

He followed the path, never really noticing how weird the swamp looked this day, never seeing the trees he walked among. He swatted at a particularly huge mosquito, was impressed at the great smear of blood it left on his forearm, but continued, single-minded as ever. In a little while, on a point of high ground above the spread of Fanner's Creek, he could see someone standing, moving near the edge of the water which was flowing swiftly even here in the midst of the swamp through which it filtered. Stopping so that he could look into the crisscross of green and yellow fronds that partially blocked his view, he stood and watched. It was the nigger woman.

As he looked, she stood on the bank, peering into the water. She had a long pole in her hands, and she was using it to probe the creek. The section of wood looked almost as if it could overbalance her and take her into the creek. He hoped not, since he wanted to shoot her.

Taking his pistol from his holster, he crept forward, itching to send a slug tearing through her black body. He was ready.

The dead man was gone, but the image of the white man drowning in Fanner's Creek still burned in Addie Lacher's mind.

She could see him struggling to stay afloat, and she had seen the place at which he would pass closest to shore before he went down for the last time. So she had gone to that place, a spit of high ground jutting into the creek's flow; Addie took up a spot close to the water so that she could try to snag him when he'd float by.

He was coming, any moment now, and she would do her best to save him.

Addie wasn't certain who he was, for the dead man hadn't shown her. But it didn't matter. She had never turned away from one of her visions, and she wouldn't do so today. Nearby, something called out with a high whistling sound she had never heard--she supposed it was some kind of bird, but as strange in its way as the trees and plants she had passed on her way into the swamp.

She supposed it was all part of a larger vision, although something quite different from anything she had ever experienced, but there was something about it all--something very real. Any other time, Addie would have turned to look into the trees to see what had made the sound, but she was afraid she would miss her chance to save the man if she did that. So she continued to watch.

Behind her, Mark Kiser had crept silently to a point less than a dozen feet from her. He supposed that he should go ahead and shoot her. She would never know what had hit her. But he wanted to see what she was doing. At first he had supposed that she was fishing, but the pole she was holding was much too bulky to be for fishing. And the way she was holding it out, as if to snag something passing by. He wanted to see.

Then, he'd kill her.

After his tenth attempt at making landfall, Davis wisely decided to rest and try again when the current might bring him close enough to make a grab for a jutting limb or branch dangling over the creek. For now, it was taking all his strength just to take in an occasional lungful of air before the current tumbled him about like the rest of the river detritus it tossed ahead of itself.

Davis knew that the creeks produced small side currents the locals called *old woman's' pockets* where heavy objects washed out of the main streambed to be caught on the banks. It was often where drowned bodies turned up, but he held onto the hope that he would not end up like that. He continued to kick and waited to be deposited in one of the pockets.

Going up for another breath of air, he looked back, along the way the current had taken him. He saw a slick black form cutting the surface, a thick tail driving a long body and triangular head in his direction. About thirty yards distant, Davis figured it to be a large alligator, but there was something about it that didn't look quite right. It was the wrong color, and the texture of its hide was smooth and sleek rather than the armor of a 'gator. He thought it was funny to be making such an analysis while something huge approached to probably eat him. The situation sank home.

Davis began to scream, and to thrash his arms about, kicking wildly in a vain attempt to break out of the rush of water so that he could make shore.

The thrashing of the prey before it only succeeded in spurring the hunter into action. Closing the flaps of flesh over its small nostrils, it exhausted air from bladders and submerged.

With a single stroke of its short, powerful tail, it arrowed toward the object of its desire.

Kiser had moved to within six feet of Addie when he decided that he didn't know what in Hell's name the woman was doing. It was time to just shoot her and get it over with. He was lifting his pistol into position and had glanced one last time toward the water when he heard Davis Ryan's screams of anger. He turned to see.

Addie Lacher, too, had heard Ryan's screams. But she had also sensed Kiser as he crept upon her. Slowly, but more quickly than Kiser had a right to expect, she spun her body three hundred degrees, grasping the cypress pole as tightly as she could. The hard, water polished wood struck Kiser at his right temple, not hard enough to knock him unconscious, but hard enough so that he fell into the water at the verge of Fanner's Creek.

While Kiser choked and struggled to keep himself from being swept away by the current, Addie waited as Davis' thrashing form came closer. She repositioned herself and held out the end of the pole, hoping that Davis would get to her before Kiser could regain his footing. She had seen the gun in his hand, and she could imagine the old bastard shooting her, although she could not imagine why he would do such a thing.

Davis was almost within reach of the pole. She could see who it was. "Davis Ryan! Grab hold o' this pole! Grab it!" He was frightened, looking back in the water at something.

Kiser had reached out with his left hand and had grabbed a fistful of cypress knee jutting out of the water at the creek's edge, thereby saving himself from being washed away. Cursing, he stood up in the soft mud, the water sucking at his shins, and he drew a bead on Addie as she waited for a chance to snag the drowning man floating by. "Say goodbye, nigger bitch!"

Davis heard Addie screaming at him over his own screams. He saw the pale length of wood and grabbed for it, hoping he would not pull the old woman in with him.

The hunter sensed its warm prey very close and it thrashed four times with its muscular tail, its huge jaws wide and ready to bite down.

Davis made a grab for the pole. The weight of his body and the force of the current almost pulled Addie off of her perch.
Still, she held on and began to draw Davis to her.

Kiser's gun went off, and Addie winced, expecting to feel the slug tearing into her. She did not expect the shot to go wild as Kiser aimed drunkenly, to hear Kiser screaming in pain, screaming that something *had hold of his leg, that it was tearing his leg off, that he'd dropped his gun and wouldn't someone just make it let go!*
As Addie Lacher reached down and pulled Davis Ryan ashore, grabbing at his soaked shirt, both of them looked to where Kiser had been standing in the creek's shallows. Despite his fatigue, despite his gasping for breath, Davis raised his head to see.
Something that was definitely not an alligator had risen out of Fanner's Creek. Its great, triangular head was locked about Kiser's left leg--had bitten it clean through, in fact. Blood was streaked across its tar-black snout, even spattering its tiny, marble-sized eyes. The old police officer screamed anew as the thing swallowed and quickly bit again, this time grasping Kiser about the abdomen so that when it clamped down, the force of the action made a

fountain of blood gush out of Kiser's upturned mouth so that his scream became a gout of silent crimson.

After that, it pulled back with stubby legs and man and beast vanished in the dark current of Fanner's Creek.

Quickly, on hands and knees, Davis crawled away from the water, wanting to be far from it. Beside him, Addie helped him along.

CHAPTER TWENTY-FIVE

Pat Wilson was torn. He knew what he wanted to do, and yet he had a responsibility to go to Martinsville and get help. If he had felt he had a choice he would've gone hunting for Sage. He took one look at Michelle lying in shock in Ed Childress' house, and he knew he didn't really have a choice. Red Sage would have to wait; for now, he'd have to go for the sheriff.

With the bridge over the spur road out, there were a couple of alternatives open to him. On the west side of Woodvine, where the town ended and faded into piney groves, he could find his way out to highway on old logging roads. He had his Bronco with its new muds and four wheel drive; with that, he could handle just about anything the local countryside could throw at him.

It would be rough travel, but he'd done more than his fair share of deer hunting through that brush and he could find his way through in a couple of hours, at worst. His second choice was the old ford over Fanner's Creek; it was merely a shallow place made there by Confederate engineers in the 1860's. They had taken some slabs of granite from Thirty Acre Rock, laying them down in sandy shallows so that wagons and horses could be driven across. If the creek was up too high, then he'd have turn around and he'd be out of luck.

If not, it wouldn't take him much longer than if he still had the bridge to cross.

He made his choice.

"Ed, you keep a close watch on the ladies. Michelle's in shock, I know, and I'm not too sure about your Mary. So you keep your eyes peeled for that crazy bastard, and if you see him I want you to blow his stinkin' brains out!" Pat indicated the .45 he had taken from his house and given to Ed. It lay on the coffee table in front of

Childress, all chrome and polish. "And you don't take no chances if you see that asshole, Kiser! Or that damned Ray Weller, too! Hell, you cain't trust none of 'em.

"Now I'm goin' to head out to the old ford on Fanner's Creek. If the creek's up too high, then you'll see me headed back past the house here in about thirty minutes 'cause I'll have to turn around and go out one of them loggin' roads past Joe Gunn's house." He turned and headed for the door. "An' if you need me, then you flag me down if I'm headed back. Okay?"

"Yeah, Pat. Don't worry. You just be careful."

"I will." He was gone.

Red worked his magic for what he knew would be the final time. He knelt there on the rough surface of the huge blister of rock, and he called out just a small part of that which lay within. There was no longer a reason for what he did; he didn't need one, really. The rush of power that flowed out of the Rock and through him and into that other place was reason enough for what he did. There was glory left in Woodvine. Glory enough for all of them.

The enormous beast formed, and forces beyond Red's understanding or capacity to control were released in a great surge. Sage laughed through the thunder of the beast's mighty tread and the roar of its breast.

He couldn't believe it. Pat could not believe his luck.

Before him, sitting at the edge of the road where paths led down to Thirty Acre Rock was the Woodvine Police car. Pat knew that wherever that car was, Red was nearby. He could keep going until he came to the ford and then make his way to Martinsville.

Or he could stop here, find Sage and save them all a lot of trouble. Try as he might, he could not get the image of Davis lying at the bottom of Fanner's Creek out of his mind.

Martinsville could wait. He hit the brakes and skidded to a halt in the wet, sandy road. *Time for payback.*

Climbing out of the Bronco, Pat strode quickly over to the police cruiser and put his hand on the hood. It was still warm, but not hot, so Red had obviously parked it some time ago. But not too long ago. He shouldn't be hard to locate. If he was somewhere out there on the Rock, then Pat would have no trouble finding him. No trouble, at all.

Going back to the Bronco, he opened the door and climbed in to retrieve the rifle he'd brought with him. He had chosen the 30.06, since that was what Davis had suggested he take when they had gone searching for the Wishons. He grabbed up his rucksack, too: full of ammo. And if he'd bothered to have looked, he would have seen the small item Red Sage had left there while he had slept off his storm-inspired drunk. Instead, he took it with him.

In the soft sand of the path that led away from the road, Pat looked down and saw the shoeprints Sage had left. He was sure it was Sage, now, for the prints were from Sage's dress shoes; the kind the asshole always wore regardless of where he was or what he was doing. Pat cradled his rifle in the crook of his right arm and plunged down the path. He had a feeling that this wouldn't take long.

As he moved down the path, he kept his eyes glued to the ground, watching to make certain that Sage had not veered from the trail and gone into the woods or onto one of the fingers of rock where it would have been harder for Pat to find him. But Sage had continued on the trail, merely following it to where it terminated at the widest part of the Rock, where Fanner's Creek cut through the hard stone like a slow, insistent knife.

Thinking of his best friend being struck from behind, being left to drown in the swollen creek, Pat could think only of revenge. His only intention was to let Sage know what was going to happen to him before he pulled the trigger and blew his guts out. Thinking of that, he found himself racing down the path, no longer caring whether or not he was able to steal upon the bastard who had murdered Davis.

Coming out of the trees, away from the sparse limbs that slapped at his face and left him wet with the previous night's rain, Pat found himself looking out on the broad expanse of Thirty Acre Rock. The sun beamed down a bit hotter than he would have thought; waves of heat flittered before him, warping the view of the trees on the far side of the Rock. He blinked, not understanding what he was seeing. Was that a man over there, beyond the cut of the creek? What had that surge of movement been at the edge of the forest just as he'd broken from the trees?

He walked out onto the Rock itself, meaning to cross over to where he could get a better look at the man, and to shoot him if it was Sage.

Moving out over the granite, Pat walked to within thirty feet of the gap that marked Fanner's Creek. Once there, he raised his rifle to his shoulder and peered down the length of his scope. He moved along the line of the ground until he focused in on the figure on the other side. It was Sage, all right. What in the name of Heaven was he doing? Sage looked at him. A sound came at Pat from that direction. A strange sound. Feeling dizzy, he looked up.

He blinked, not understanding what he was seeing.

Something...something red hovered over him, spinning like a top above his head. It seemed to grow there in the air, just out of reach, spinning and growing as it seemed to become more and more solid. All around him, sound seemed to have been swallowed up: he could hear nothing--not his own breath, not his heartbeat, not the sound of his feet atop the granite. He could only stand and stare at the ropy thing as it danced above him. It seemed almost solid enough to touch. He reached up.

And as his hand made as if to touch it, the form ceased to spin and came down, as if melting into him, becoming part of him. He heard someone laughing. It was Red Sage, and Pat remembered why he was there. Time to shoot someone.

Even as the rifle came up to his shoulder, Pat heard the blast of the beast's roar. There was actually a shock wave as the noise rocked physically into him. The surprise of it caused him to pause, to look into the direction from which it had come. He saw.

For something so terribly large, it exploded from the line of tall trees with a speed that could not be real. Its gold and red body gleamed in the sunlight, gleamed like something polished by some oriental artisan. But it was a thing of flesh, tons of flesh that propelled itself forward on gigantic legs. Pat was locked into place; he could not run and knew down deep in his mind that to do so would be a foolish thing. So he stood frozen and gazed across and up at this monster that had halved the distance between them on four great strides and would be on him in less than two seconds. If he had paused any longer he would not have been able to draw the gun to his shoulder and fire.

The gun roared back at the creature in its own little way, and Pat felt the quick recoil as he fired. The slug, large enough to stop a black bear in its track, powerful enough to atomize the heart and lungs of a full grown buck, smacked into the beast as it closed on the pasty faced man who stood his ground before it.

The only thing the beast saw was the red meat that was meant for it; all it felt was a quick stinging as the bullet entered the thick and armored flesh near its abdomen, just above the thick muscle that joined left leg to torso. After that, the bullet lodged there in the reptilian thing, merely an insignificant nettle in the enormity of its body. It hardly noticed, and it did not pause in its quick hunt.

Pat Wilson had no time to fire another shot before jaws opened and the head darted downward and teeth sheared through him. There was a small spray of blood as the beast tossed his broken body skyway, tipping its head back to catch the morsel as it fell back into its maw, there to be sheared again and swallowed.

Pat's gun clattered uselessly to the stone.

Red Sage watched, laughing, laughing. As the great beast turned, sniffing the new prey that waited to be taken, looking for the red mark that would show it the way, Sage watched and laughed.

CHAPTER TWENTY-SIX

"It's that man, Sage. He done somethin' to this town." Addie said it, speaking of it to someone for the first time.

Davis sat on the edge of her porch and rested, gathering his strength for the journey back to Woodvine. It'd be a good three mile walk just to make it back to the edges of the town. "I know who it is, but I don't know what he's done. That thing that came out of the water and killed Kiser. What was it? What is Sage doing?" He looked up at the old woman who sat in the chair where he'd last seen her.

"I don't know. I only know that he does somethin' that kills. It made that storm last night, too." She rocked and the air was filled with the light creaking of wood against wood. The breeze remained still and silent.

"Mrs. Lacher, you know I've got to get back to town. I don't want to leave you here, but I've got to go back before something really bad happens again." He knew he couldn't carry her, and she was too old to make the walk with him. This, he knew. But she had saved his life and he did not want to leave her. The idea of leaving her alone disgusted him.

"You don't worry about me, Davis Ryan. Somebody has got to stop him before he does it again. There's been a lot of people killed the last few days. I can see 'em in my dreams. If you want to do me some good, you stop him so I don't see them people no more. You do that for me." She rocked, and around them the breeze was picking up, beginning to just tug at the smallest leaves on the trees.

"I don't have a gun to leave you."

"Don't need no gun. Never had one, an' don't want one."

"I feel bad about leaving you here." He was standing, preparing to leave anyway.

"You ain't got any choice. So you best be gone." She looked up, and saw that a few anemic clouds were beginning to mar the amazingly blue sky: a handful of cotton streaks across azure.

"I had a dream about something, Davis. I dreamed about a storm worse than the one last night. An' my dreams always tell me about somethin' that happens." The first gust of the day actually made rushing sounds through the palmetto. "You better go, an' you better go, now."

Davis stood, walked a few steps away from her little porch.

"I'll be back for you as soon as I can, Addie. I'll be back before it gets dark."

She managed a smile for him. "I'll be here. I'll wait for you." There was an icy fear in her heart as she waved him on.

"Now, get. Get!"

He went up the path that led away from her house, walking where water had receded in the minutes since she had saved his life. Watching him go, she noticed that he did not look back at her; there was too much guilt in him, and he did not want to see her sitting old and alone on that porch. Addie smiled. She liked him for it.

"Great God!" He couldn't believe his luck. There at the end of the road, where Kiser had left it, was the wagon he had driven to Addie Lacher's house. He went around to the driver's side, and had to squeezed past a stand of Spanish bayonet, careful not to get pricked on the sharp spines there. But he had seen the thing that came out of the water dragging Kiser down. Surely the man had carried his keys with him. Davis slapped his pockets and found that he still had Ed's keys with him. Not that they'd do him any good. He opened the door of Kiser's truck.

"You cocky bastard!" The keys were there, dangling from the steering column where the old police officer had left them. "Didn't think anyone was going to drive off with your car, did you?" Davis climbed in, sat back for a second and closed his eyes.

He was tired, very tired; as tired as he'd ever been. There wasn't time to relax, though. Davis didn't know what Sage was up to. There was no rhyme or reason to the things that had been happening around Woodvine, and none of it made sense to him. In fact, he found it hard to come to grips with any of it. Sage couldn't make a storm come up out of nowhere; no man could control the weather.

And why would he want to kill the people of Woodvine? Why had he sent Kiser to do away with old Mrs. Lacher? She'd told Davis that she could see the future, that she knew what Red was up to. He couldn't believe that, but she had been there with that pole to save him. And what had that thing been that had crawled out of Fanner's Creek after Kiser, the thing that had been (he shivered) stalking him for the last mile of his near drowning? He started the car and pressed down on the gas with his stockinged foot.

Putting the car into reverse, he twisted in his seat to make sure that he wouldn't hit anything when he turned around.

"Oh, you S.O.B.! Thank you!" Lying on the back seat was Kiser's twelve gauge. It was a double barreled job, the one Pat

Wilson was always drooling over when talk turned to local guns.

Pat had tried to buy it from Kiser many times in the past, but the old bastard never would let go of the antique. There was a box of shells on the seat next to the gun--slugs. Glancing quickly about, he gave the wagon the gas and spun around in the wet sand. He headed toward Woodvine.

He went too fast through the piney woods back to the edge of town, taking too many chances on the curves and flooring the auto as he took it across hard washboard. Davis didn't care. It wasn't his car and the owner wasn't going to complain. And all he could think about was Michelle. If Sage had done anything to Michelle, he didn't know what he'd do. He didn't want to hang around if she wasn't there to be with. "Fuck you, Red. I'm coming for your ass!"

The wagon picked up speed, hurtling down the sandy road.

Passing Fred Chappel's farm, Davis did not pause to stop, only jerked his head in the general direction of the white frame house that he had seen only the week before. It was still there.

And why shouldn't it be? He thought of John and Beth's garage, realizing that something besides the wind had knocked it down. The image of those pale marks high on the pines behind the Martin house came back to him, too. What the hell was going on?

And soon, he came out of the wall of pulpwood trees and slash pines, seeing familiar houses and coming on the pocked surface of the spur road. The station wagon met the pavement, the nose jumping high as the front tires actually left the ground for an instant. There was a screech of steel and a spray of orange sparks as it came back down. Someone peeked from behind drawn curtains at Joe Gunn's house, then Davis sped by his own home and despite it all he thought about a pair of boots sitting in his bedroom.

He was doing eighty when he passed Michelle's house and had only slowed to sixty when the Childress home came into view and he slammed on the brakes sending a cloud of burned rubber continuing on in the increasing wind. Getting out, his nose was assailed by the stench of cooked tires, but he hardly noticed. He flew across the lawn and raced up Ed and Mary's front steps.

Ed met him at the front door, a pistol in his hand--the one that Michelle had been left with.

"Davis! Davis, I don't believe it! I thought you were dead!" He was brandishing the pistol, pointing it at Davis without thinking of what he was doing.

"God, Ed, don't point that thing at me!" He put out his hand and edged it away from his body.

"Oh. I'm sorry, Davis. When I saw the wagon, I thought you were Kiser." He pointed with his free hand at the car sitting skewed in the road.

"No. We don't have to worry about Kiser anymore." Davis pushed past Ed, into the house, looking intently.

"What do you mean? What happened?"

But Davis didn't have time to explain anything. "Where's Michelle, Ed? Is she okay?"

"Uh. Yeah. I mean, she's out. I gave her one of Mary's sedatives. She thinks you're dead, Davis. I told her what happened, and she just went crazy. She went running over to Pat

Wilson's house screaming that you were dead and..."

Davis was moving again, into the house. "Which bedroom?"

"There. In there, where Mary is. We put them together. So I could watch them, you know?" Ed went ahead and opened the door to the bedroom. On well-oiled hinges, the door swung soundlessly inward and a long rectangle of light illuminated the room. Both of the women dozed on the wide surface of the bed, a lacy white afghan fading to yellow beneath them.

Davis stood in the door and looked down on Michelle, loving her. "I should wake her. I should wake her and tell her that I'm okay. Shouldn't I?"

Uncharacteristically, Ed pulled Davis away from the door and shut it quietly. "I don't know, Davis," he hissed. "Pat says that Michelle's in shock. I don't think we ought to bother her until she sleeps that medicine out. I just don't think it would be good."

"Yeah. I reckon you're right." He looked back toward the doorway, into the daylight that was growing dimmer. "Storm's comin'," he said.

"What?"

"Like last night. Storm's comin' back like last night, only worse." He sighed, looking down at his feet and wishing he had a pair of shoes.

"What are you talking about?" Ed led him away from the door, seeing that Davis was covered in sand and mud and bit of rotted vegetation from his plunge. "How do you know it's going to storm again? The sun was just shining?"

"Addie Lacher told me. She said it was going to come up worse than it was last night. I think she's right." He went all the way back to the front door.

"Where is Pat? Where did he go when he left here?"

Childress stared at the floor, feeling useless, as if he had been no help to anyone. "He took his Bronco and said he was going to go to Martinsville. Said he'd go up to the ford and get across there, and if he couldn't make it there, then he'd go out the back way; you know, down them loggin' roads."

"Yeah. I know. How long ago was that?"

"About two hours. He didn't head back this way. I've been watchin', so he must've got across the ford."

"Yeah. He must've." He thought about Red Sage, knowing that Pat would take a crack at the bastard, if he'd gotten the chance.

"Anybody seen Red? I mean, since he kicked me in the head and tried to kill me."

Now Childress looked as if he were staring a hole in the floor. "Not since...not since he left here."

"Left here! What are you talking about?" Davis glared at Ed.

"He, uh, he brought me back here...you know, afterwards."

"Christ, Ed!" Davis raised his arms in exasperation and let them fall to his sides. "Shit." He sighed. "Where did he go after that? Did you see?"

"That way. Back toward..."

Davis stared back in the direction of the east side of town, where Pat would have had to go if he were going to try the ford. "Shit! Pat went that way!" Ryan clattered down the stairs, making too much noise.

"You watch after Michelle! You stay right here and watch Michelle and don't you let anything happen to her! You hear me? If you so much as see Red, you blow his head off!" Davis paused long enough to point his finger at Ed.

"I hear you," Childress said, retreating into his house and closing the door, this time locking it.

The wagon's tires screeched into the growing wind and the neighbors could smell the burnt stuff on the air.

CHAPTER TWENTY-SEVEN

Red Sage sat in his office. He had taken a hammer and had pulled out the nails that held the windows shut. The room had been alive with the painful sound of nails coming free of wood. Red imagined he heard people coming in and out of offices and anterooms. He thought he heard footsteps in the hallway, judges coming to talk to him, police officers coming to ask his advice, friends coming to visit. Going from one window to the next, he had extricated all of the nails and had pulled down the musty tarps that covered the glass, and he had thrown wide the windows, letting in the air and giving himself the best view of Woodvine in town.

It was all but dead.

A tear felt its way down his face as he leaned against the sill and looked upon his city. It had been a grand place in its day. Now he could see empty storefronts and empty streets and weed-grown lots--he owned several of the empty plots, had had plans for them in his day. That one across the street from the gas station had been bought to build another car lot for the expansion of Benny Pyle's Chevrolet dealership. "Goddamned cowards." Pyle had left years and years ago, emptying his bank accounts and retiring to Arizona.

There was a line of shops across the street from the lot, facing it. He had owned all or part of half a dozen businesses there, had spent thousands of dollars buying out partners who had left for greener pastures or who had died and left good-for-nothing children behind who had run rather than stayed and made a go of it. "You cowards!" He leaned out of the window and screamed into the empty streets that radiated around and out from the city building. They were gone, most of them. But some were left. Some were left to witness the end.

He first heard, then saw Kiser's station wagon speeding up the spur road from the far side of town. When it had drawn to within two blocks of the city hall, he could see that it wasn't Kiser who drove the car. Even from here he could see Davis Ryan's angry face glaring up at him. "Well, I'll be damned," he whispered.

The wagon jumped the curb, sideswiping the squad car he had parked below. "That's all right, Davis. Maybe I didn't finish you off, but it's too late for you. It's too late for all of you. Come on up. We'll talk a while."

There was a crash as Davis shoved the door inward; plaster fell from the wall when the brass knob smacked into it. "Red, you bastard!"

"Davis." Sage sat in his chair, leaning back comfortably and looking not at all worried. Atop his desk was an open cloth sack. There was a spill of leather patches strewn out of it, red paint staining the wood where it glowed fresh and wet. Ryan's gaze centered there, and he squinted in confusion, not knowing what he was seeing. And then his eyes fell upon the shattered gun that he recognized as Pat's. Sage saw that he'd seen it, and indicated with a nod. "Like my trophy?"

"Where's Pat, Red? Where is he?"

"Dead. Quite dead. A friend of mine ate him." He smiled.

A chill went through Davis then. He knew, somehow, that Red was not lying. "You bastard, I'm going to kill you." He realized that he had left the shotgun in the back seat of Kiser's wagon.

Davis would have to take Red on with his bare hands, and he wasn't at all sure that he could do that, even if he wasn't wrung out from the ordeal he had already suffered through. He took a step across the room.

There was a metallic click, and the pistol appeared over the lip of the desk in Red's left hand. Red's sleeves were rolled up and his fingers were stained with crimson paint. "Don't make me shoot you, Davis. You know I'd be happy to. But why do that when we can talk? Be reasonable and you'll live longer. Is it a deal?"

Davis stared at the barrel of the gun. He could try dodging aside.

Red cocked the trigger back. "I asked you for a deal."

He swallowed and answered Sage. "Yeah. Deal."

"Fine. I knew you'd listen to reason." Sage leaned back a bit further and propped his long legs on the desktop. He kept the gun aimed at Davis, but felt secure enough to look out the window, as if watching for something. Far and away, there came a low sound, barely heard.

"Red, what are you doing? What in God's name are you up to?" Davis stood and felt tired, felt as if he would have a hard time standing there for long. He knew he must look like an easy mark for Red, with or without that gun. His stockinged feet were stinging and bleeding from a dozen cuts, his legs were impossibly tired, and the wet clothes were beginning to chafe him raw at his knees and armpits. But if he fell, it would just make Red laugh at him, and might give him an excuse to go ahead and shoot. No. He'd stand there and wait for his chance.

"Oh, you stupid man. You can't imagine what I'm doing, can you? What I've done, what remains to be done. But have a little patience and you'll soon..." Red tilted his head toward the window and looked out, peering through the corners of his eyes without turning his face away from Davis. "...see." Outside, still far away but closer, he heard a heavy thumping.

"See what?" Oh, Davis Ryan was tired. He held on, thinking of Michelle, seeing Pat's rifle, bent and scratched and stained with something red going to brown (not paint).

"I want you to see how this town deserves to die. Not long and slow. That's too painful, and I'm sick of dying like that, of watching my town go to the grave in long...slow...stages.

"I'm sick of it!"

There was a vague crashing sound: like wood going to splinters somewhere blocks away.

Davis flicked his own head toward the window, looking at the sky and the town. Clouds blocked all the blue in the sky, now. "What is that? What is it, Red?"

Sage smiled, wistfully, sadly. "I'm not sure what it is,

Davis. I have to tell you that I don't know what it is, for sure. I've seen drawings of things that look like it, but they've been gone from this world for a long, long time." He chuckled, cleared his throat. The splintering sound continued. "Beth Wilkins' place."

"What?"

"It sounds like it's at Beth Wilkins' place." He looked back to Davis. "Don't try to get any closer. I know you want to try. But don't. I'll kill you." Davis shifted his foot back, leaving a red smear on the floor.

"Woodvine doesn't deserve to die like it was," Sage continued. "So I decided to take matters into my own hands.

"I've known about this thing since '39. Since '39!" He seemed to be looking right through Davis, into another place somewhere beyond Ryan. "This little brown man came into town, asking about Thirty Acre Rock. *Little foreign nigger*. That's what Kiser called him before he ran him in for vagrancy. The fellow was quite surprised by Kiser's brutality. Didn't know what he was getting into here in this country, I reckon.

"When Kiser mentioned the strange man to me, I had to see him. You know, I really was just curious to talk to him. And I had every intention of just releasing him and taking him out of town and letting him go back to wherever it was he was from--Asia, Africa, maybe.

"But he was too smart for his own good. He wanted to deal. He told me that he wanted to see Thirty Acre Rock because he claimed it was one of Earth's *eternal points*!" Sage chuckled. "Can you imagine? Hell, I didn't know what he was talking about then, and I don't know now. But I wanted to know. So I got Kiser to unlock the cell, and I took him out to the Rock one night.

"And he showed me something, Davis. He showed me how to do something you would not believe." The muffled crashing sound stopped and was followed by that horrible thumping. "The strange thing about it was that, as I watched him, I knew that I could do it better than he could. It...it's how you*think* , Davis! It's all in how you look at the world when you're calling it up. And I don't think he realized it, until it was too late. Until right before I shot him dead." The thumping sound was coming closer. It was almost loud.

"But just calling it up, that's not all. It can't be controlled. Not truly. But it can be led." Sage held up his bare arm, and Davis could see a strange letter painted there on Red's still muscular forearm. It looked oriental, somehow. "It can be led about like a bull with a nose ring, if you put one of these somewhere; some place where there's warm meat nearby."

Davis stared now with some fear at the window. The noise was very loud, getting louder. He could see nothing but the wind stirring ever stronger, blowing leaves through the air. "Red, what are you saying? You ain't making any sense at all!"

"It's the mark here, Ryan. If you give somebody one of these, it makes it think that they're its food, that they're whatever it eats in whatever place it calls home!" Something crashed nearby and the two heard metal spilling onto pavement. "It's coming across Sullivan's junk lot. Be here soon." And Davis saw something moving over Sage's head, something tenuous and crimson spinning slowly in the air there.

"Red...what in God's name..." Davis swallowed and watched, not understanding.

"The mark makes it think people are prey. If the mark is nowhere nearby, then it ignores you. Or it did when I was around to send it back. I don't know what'll happen now."

Davis had seen a machine on the highway once. It had been a huge contraption hammering thick wooden posts into the ground for construction of a guard rail. The ground had shook around that machine much the same as it did now--only not as much.

"Red, what is happening?"

"It's coming, Davis! Oh, it's a glorious thing! And when I don't send it back, it'll raze this town to the bare ground. It's a hugry beast, Davis. We'll be lunch, and it'll crave for more!"

Red was standing, and despite what knowledge he had, there was fear in him. He stared out the window and ignored Davis.

"They'll come from everywhere, Davis! Ah, the Atlanta Journal will be writing about us for a year! And every television in every home will play us like a song! It'll be grand!" The city hall shook at its very foundations. A great, black shadow spilled across the street from the direction the two men could not look.

There was an instant of silence. The thing glowing over Sage ceased its dance and came slowly down and merged with his body.

The reptilian head that appeared at the window was too large to fit through it, so the mortar sprayed inward in a shower of stones and broken glass as the muzzle forced itself through. Above the din of destruction, Davis heard Red screaming. "I'll see you in Hell, Davis!"

Ryan fell back, himself screaming unintelligibly, wanting to be away from the impossible thing that sheared Red Sage in half and wolfed down his broken rag doll of a body. It turned toward Davis.

But already, Davis was backpedaling, making his way through the wide door he had entered. Turning his back on the thing, he made his way toward the stairs. As he raced down them, he heard an awful crashing, and knew that the entire wall on that side of the building was giving way. If he could not escape, then the thing would have him as surely as it had Red Sage.

At the bottom of the stair was another door that had been closed and chained. There was still a red crowbar stationed next to a glass fronted fire extinguisher there. Ryan grasped the bar and shoved it between one of the links. The wall at his back began to shatter; it was there, trying to get at him. He pushed the crowbar down and pried. The wall cracked, showering him with plaster dust. There was a roar that defied description, that warned everyone left in town. The shock of it almost knocked Davis off his feet. The chain gave.

Ryan swung the door wide and threw himself down the narrow stairwell there. He pounded down the close walled descent, going into the shadowed, webbed place. There was another crashing, and he knew the wall where he had been had given way. It was clawing at the door where he had just entered. Ryan went to the basement and he cowered in the very gut of the building, where there was just a small, cramped space that no one had been in for fifteen years. Spider webs fell drily about him, but he did not notice. He lay curled and cowering while the thing raged and clawed at the too narrow concrete way above his head.

After what seemed a long, long time, it stopped. Ryan waited.

Above, the thing gave up on the tenacious morsel it could not quite reach. It pointed its great snout to the wind, sniffed once and was away, pounding on pillar legs.

As the tread of the thing receded, Davis rose up, thinking of Michelle. He went to the wagon and loaded the shotgun. He had to go after it.

CHAPTER TWENTY-EIGHT

Addie watched the weird trees lifting slowly above the horizon of green piney growth she had known for all of her life.

They were strange things, like trees she had never seen. There were greens, yes, but of shades and texture that were totally unfamiliar to her. Fronds uncurled above the withering shortleaf and slash pines that had grown in rows down to the damp outlines of Fanner's Swamp. Crowns of waxy yellows and reds dappled the vague colors of the planted evergreens, slowly outdoing them as she watched, her eyes becoming heavy with drowsiness. The swamp was changing, the land was changing, giving way to something else.

She hoped that Davis Ryan would return for her very soon. Addie was frightened, fearing the awful animal she had seen in her dreams. It would not do for her to sleep. Not now. Her eyelids fluttered with fatigue, her old head nodding down to her thin chest.

Her eyes snapped open and her head whipped up.

The dead man was at her feet. He was reaching out to her, his brown fingers just touching her forehead. She felt the tips of his fingers brush the skin above her brow.

Addie gaped wide at what she was seeing. It was the Rock. She recognized the place, although she had not seen it since she was still a young woman. But familiar though it was, it was as unlike any place she had ever seen as the strange trees that were slowly appearing in the woods around her house. There were still many of the familiar pines but the post and water oaks had disappeared.

The palmetto and bear grass and Spanish bayonet were gone. There were only weird plants and scaled trunks rising in the black earth all around the Rock. And the Rock itself was open, as a door might open, and out of it was pouring things should not be, things that had died a long, long time ago and which should remain dead.

She could see armored leather, heaving with humid life; she could see claws and great teeth waiting beyond the door, ripping and gnashing for the moment when some last membrane would tear and let them through.

And then she was seeing the dead man again. He was standing still in front of her, touching the spot above her eyes. With a great effort, he seemed to take a breath, as through a wounded lung, as in air that was too thin to breathe. His mouth was a small round hole that labored awfully. After a time, he spoke, and this time Addie truly heard his voice with her ears.

"It must be stopped. The great beast must be killed."

She felt his breath feather across the bridge of her nose.

Addie blinked.

The dead man was gone. But the forest had changed even more.

There were now less of oaks and even the pines were crowded by strangely colored waxy fronds. Going first to the kitchen where she took a long drink of water, she grabbed up her walking staff, descended to her yard and made her way down the path toward Woodvine. Perhaps she would find Davis Ryan. And perhaps he could kill the thing before it was too late.

Perhaps.

Something that large could not have disappeared so quickly and yet it had.

Davis had forced his way out of the tumble of broken walls and shattered beams that had been the south side of the city hall. For a moment, he had feared that he would not be able to escape, that he had been trapped in the basement where he had taken refuge. Squeezing through a last tumble of splinters and mortar, he felt his way clear so that he was at last able to wriggle free and into fresh air. The growing wind had picked at his graying hair, pulling at it and letting him know that another storm was on its way just as Addie Lacher had warned. He went around the ruined building to where he had parked Kiser's wagon, hoping it had not been destroyed by the towering monster that had brought the building down on him. The car sat unmolested precisely where he had left it.

Looking up the street and down, he could see nothing moving except for the odd bits of leaves that were being blown about by the growing wind. No great reptilian head reared above the low buildings that made up the old downtown of Woodvine. Nothing shook the earth, grinding down with tons-heavy tread.

Warily, afraid to turn his back on the world, Davis limped over to the wagon and opened the back door, reaching in for the shotgun he had left there. It lay partially on the floorboard, amidst gray carpeting and a spill of shells. He picked up the gun, fingered the red shells and slowly loaded them into the weapon.

Kiser must have been thinking of hunting deer or bear, or perhaps he had bought the ammo out of plain meanness; for the shells were twelve gauge slugs--pure discs of solid metal that could plow into flesh and liquefy it. Such ammunition could stop a bear in its tracks or turn a buck's organs to jelly. But he didn't know what they would do against something as large and as powerful as what he had seen. That thing was as big as twenty bears.

He stood, feeling exhausted, his legs wracked with fatigue, his feet bloody and stinging. It would take cannon to fight such a creature; it would take a tank to do battle with it. The smart thing to do would be to take advantage of the fact that the thing was nowhere to be seen and get the hell out of Woodvine. Just get Michelle and bull his way down the logging roads until he could break clear onto the freeway. That's what he should do.

That's what he would do.

CHAPTER TWENTY-NINE

Davis craned his neck, trying to see around the long curve that led down to his own side of town, trying to see past the houses that did not hold Michelle. Guiltily, all he could think of was escaping, of stopping only long enough to snatch her up and get away from doomed Woodvine. He pushed down on the pedal until it all but touched the floorboard, not caring that someone might step out from behind some tree or some wall of shrubbery to die on the hood of Kiser's auto. He kept thinking of that living wall of pebbled skin looming outside the window of Red's office. He kept thinking of the great dinosaur head that had shoved its way in, cutting Sage in half and swallowing his spurting body. Too bad for the others. Too bad.

His tires screamed over uneven pavement as he neared what had been the Wilkins' house. The former two-story building now lay nearly flat, a mash of broken planks and jutting beams. A little brown dog sniffed at the verge of the mess, halting for a moment to look up as Davis sped by. He didn't even want to stop and see if anyone yet lived in the jumble of woody trash the thing had left behind. No. No one had survived. The Wilkins' house didn't even have a basement.

Ahead, he saw something lying in the roadway, and he was forced to slow down so that he did not collide with it. Davis eased his foot off of the accelerator, veered to the right and thereby avoided what had been a truck: a '63 Chevy, he saw, and more likely than not belonging to Wesley Jarman. He thought he saw something red splashed across the road on the far side, but he couldn't be certain. He sped on.

Ed and Mary Childress' house was just ahead of him, less than half a mile up. Someone else's house was gone, he noted, trying not to think of familiar faces. The wagon bounced over a pothole he would've avoided any other time, and the car made a pained ratcheting sound as metal met pavement once, twice. Something began to taptaptap in the undercarriage. Davis floored it again.

Only a copse of big chestnut oaks hid the Childress home from view. Davis was actually doing seventy-five as he swung the car about, hit the brakes and left a half chalk, half tarry cloud of stinking smoke wafting on toward the far side of town. Wide eyed, his knuckles white on the steering wheel, he stared at Ed and Mary's house.

It was untouched.

Smelling the stench of burned tire rubber as he leaped out of the car, Davis stumbled across the yard and went up the stairs to the front porch; he left rusty footprints on the blue finish Ed had painted on the porch weeks before. He barely noted the painful stinging in the soles of his feet. "Ed! Ed, I'm back! We need to get the Hell out of here! Ed! Get Michelle and Mary!" He roared into the darkness of the house.

For an overlong moment, there was no reply, only the muttering of the engine in Kiser's wagon and the dark hallway staring back at him. And the rising wind through the trees.

"Ed? Ed!"

Somewhere, a door squeaked opened and he heard Ed Childress talking back. "Davis!" He was coming out of the shadows toward the other man who stood in the light at the front door. "You don't know what we've seen, Davis! God! We thought it was coming here! But it didn't! It kept right on going, right past." Ed's voiced had faded suddenly to a whisper as he gazed back the way Davis had come. "It...it was running after Wesley Jarman. He was in his truck and he--he couldn't outrun it, Davis. I...I think it caught up with him. I heard something. A crash, I think."

"Look, Ed." Ryan was gripping Childress, holding him tightly by the shoulders, trying to give him something solid to look at, but feeling soft, ready to give way himself. "We can't stay here. You saw what it is, how big it is. If it wants us, then there's nothing we can do around here to stop it. We have to get out of Woodvine, then we can think about getting some help to the rest."

Ed's eyes lit up. "Leave! Yes!"

"You have to get Mary. We have to get Mary and Michelle and we've got to hit the road now. Don't..."

thmp.

He felt it. The earth vibrated, sent tiny tremors up the foundation of the house and into the very boards on which they stood.

"Don't waste any..."

thump.

Childress' eyes were wide and staring, and Davis could not mistake the fear painted on Ed's face, wondering if it were a reflection of his own. "Don't waste any more time," he rasped at his friend. "Goddamn it, now you go and get the ladies. You get 'em now."

As Ed scurried toward the bedroom, Davis turned back to the front door and went to the screen there. Outside, the wind was picking up, beginning to toss heavier bits into the air, gusting and sending up dry clouds of fine sand. He peered suspiciously at the line of trees across the street. Nothing stirred the pines there.

Thump!

It was getting closer. But slowly, as if taking its time, stalking rather than running amok. If they hurried...

"Davis! Help me, here. Michelle's awake, but Mary won't come to. She's way under. I gave her a hell of a dose." In the hallway, Ed was partially hidden by a shadow, and Michelle stood just in front of him on slightly unsteady legs, looking somewhat disoriented. Ryan went to her.

"Oh!" She was surprised at the sensation of his hand squeezing hers, almost too hard: his relief tinged with the panic that was growing in him. Michelle peered at him through her drugged haze. "Davis." The last syllable hissed into oblivion.

"You're here. You're not..." She put her hand to her eyes, as if she were squinting into the sun. "You're not dead." Her arms were about him, hugging him tighter than he would've thought.

"I love you, Davis. Don't you leave me again." Her voice was a whisper, betraying her weakness.

"I won't. I won't."

Thump Thump!

"Help me, Davis! Help me with Mary!" Spurred by the obvious approach of the thing, Ed had grabbed his wife up in his arms and was trying to carry her into the hallway. But he was too old for the task and realized that he would drop her before he got her into the car.

"Here, Ed. Let her feet down and take her arm," he placed her right arm about Ed's shoulder, "and I'll take this one and we'll walk her out." And he had Michelle by the elbow, leading her.

"How about you, Michelle? Can you walk alright?"

"I can manage," she told him.

They were already walking, going to the front door to

Kiser's wagon which continued to mutter to itself in the middle of the street. Across the way, Davis noticed a curtain come up, then quickly down as someone watched them. He felt guilty, as if he should not be running away with so many left to themselves with no one to help them. He shoved the screen door open with his left foot, noticing the pain in the soles of his feet and wincing at the sting.

Something moved from his right, just outside the door on the front porch, and it had hold of his shoulder before he could do more than call out. "Jesus!"

"Where are you people goin'?" Addie Lacher pulled at his tattered shirt and glared at Davis. She looked angry at him for all of his fatigue, in spite of her own. The ancient woman had walked all the way through the pines to Ed's house, the wagon's motor covering her arrival.

"What the hell?" Childress' eyes were wide and white, staring in surprised horror. Addie would've laughed.

"Where are you goin'," she asked again, using Ryan's arm to steady herself.

Davis looked down on the tiny woman, feeling more guilt well up in him. "We're leaving, Addie. We're getting out of Woodvine while we can still get out."

Thump! Something crashed in the pines. A mile away. Maybe more.

"You come on with us. You climb in with us and we'll all get out of here!" He edged toward the stairs, prodding Ed to do the same.

"Then what about them?" Addie pointed at people peering fearfully from parted curtains. Davis recognized the faces. "There are a hundred people in this town cain't get out 'fore that thing comes back this way."

Somewhere, small pines were shunted aside. They could hear them snap, even above the bursts of gusty wind.

"You gots to kill it, Davis Ryan."

Ed looked back to Ryan. There was fear in his face that was threatening to turn to sheer panic and Davis could see it coming. Then Ed would be no good for any of them. "Davis? Davis, what is she talking about? Aren't we getting out of here?"

"Move!" He went on, almost leaving Ed behind, almost carrying Mary down the steps by himself. "Just get your ass in gear and help me get the ladies into the damn car! Move," he roared.

Quickly, Ed and Davis placed Mary into the back seat and shoved Michelle in beside her. Mary collapsed into an unconscious heap, and Michelle lolled sluggishly beside her, not yet out of her sedated stupor.

"Davis." Ed lifted his head above the top of the car and looked across the burnished surface at Ryan. Davis peered questioningly back at him. Ed was pointing back at the house, to a point somewhere above it. "Davis, what the Hell is that?" Davis turned to look.

It hovered at a point over the thrust of the porch, twisting in the air like stringlets of blood swirling in a clear beaker of water. The sign made its obscene dance, and from too near came the terrible thunder of approaching death.

"Oh, my God," Davis whispered. He moved quickly back to the house, to where Addie Lacher waited. Davis reached out to grasp her old hand.

"You cain't do this, Davis."

The ground shook under them, actually rattling the glass in the windowpanes.

"Come on, Miz Lacher! You come on while we can get out of here!"

"You gots to kill it, Davis."

"We'll get help. Someone else will have to kill it!" He had his fingers on hers.

"There ain't time for that. There ain't time. You gots to do it!" And she pointed at him.

"I can't. I won't try. Now, are you comin' or am I gonna have to..."

Trees crashed to the ground from much too close. Something gold and brown and of pebbled surface moved through the pines. He could see it rushing toward them, partially hidden by the bulk of the house.

"It...it's here," he managed to squeak. There was a movement above his head. He looked up to see the sign descending through the tin and the wood of the roof toward the two of them.

Faintly, he heard Addie speaking to him.

"I'm buyin' you some time, Davis Ryan." There was a slight clanking noise, and he looked over to see her reaching her small, bony hand into the mailbox tacked next to the Childress' front door. She withdrew Red's patch from where he had left it. "I'm buyin' you some time, now you do what's right."

Before he could even think of trying to stop her, Addie had the crimson thing in her grasp and was holding it tight to her body. "Kill it. Kill it quick as you can so nothin' else will get out of where it comes from. If you don't, it'll all come out. It'll all come out."

And then she was scurrying away from him, away from the porch and into the yard and toward the line of green pines bowing before the stiffening wind. The red sign followed her, descending, coming down and down until she and it joined.

There was a roar, Davis watched and realized how close the thing had been to them--less than a hundred yards. He saw as it covered a distance and dipped its fanged head into the forest, stooping to find Addie. Choking, he turned and ran back to the wagon where Ed waited, frozen and staring wildly at something
Davis could not see.
Davis aimed the wagon toward the center of Woodvine and willed himself not to look to where Addie had been.

CHAPTER THIRTY

Behind them, Davis could hear the thing above the rumbling of the wagon's motor and the bothersome metallic ticking coming from somewhere in the undercarriage. The vehicle probably wouldn't take much more abuse than he had so far given it, and he wondered now if it would even have made the journey through the slash pines on rugged logging roads. It probably would not have, and he thought on that one probability and tried to convince himself that he was doing the right thing, now that Addie Lacher had sacrificed herself.

He looked across the seat at Ed Childress. The man wasn't even there, really, gone off to wherever shock takes you. Davis peered into the rear view mirror, scanning for some sign of the thing that was taking the town apart. A freshly broken bit of limb, green needles still holding on, blew from the trees and smacked wetly against the windshield. An especially hard gust thudded broadside against the wagon.

It was coming again. Addie had been right about that, so, Davis reasoned, she had also been right about something worse happening if he did not somehow kill the monster. He thought he knew how. It was worth a try, at least.

But first he had to get rid of his charges. He knew where they'd be relatively safe for a little while, even if he couldn't be certain. Still, it was all he could do under the circumstances.

At the square, he brought the wagon up to the chalky-woody ruin that had been the city hall.

Carefully, Davis pushed and heaved until he had made a respectable entrance to the stairwell that led down to the basement. It was reinforced all around with concrete and granite block and had proven too much for the horror when he'd taken refuge there, so it would probably be safe for Michelle and the Childress couple. There really wasn't another choice inside of Woodvine. Standing away from the mess, he looked down into the gloom and then went back to the car. In the back, he located a small toolbox, relieved to see that Kiser had a flashlight stored there.

Quickly, he led the three back to the hole in the ground and took them in, picking his way through the jumble of shattered beams and bricks.

"Davis?" It was Michelle, coming out of the stupor the sedatives had dropped her into.

"Yes?" He had her by the hand, leading her down first as Ed remained near the top of the stairwell with his wife, who remained unconscious through all.

"You're going to leave, aren't you? You're going to leave the three of us down here. What's going on, Davis? What's happening?" They were almost at the bottom.

"I'm not sure, Michelle. I really don't know what's happening." He wasn't lying. He felt that Addie probably had known much of what was going on, but that did them no good. And perhaps only Red truly knew what was transpiring in the dying town.

"Davis, you said you wouldn't leave me again."

They were on the floor of the basement, now. Above them, the wind was whistling through jutting two by fours, whipping at shrubbery. Davis held Michelle close to him, squeezing her tight. "I shouldn't be gone too long, Michelle. I've just got something to do. Then I'll come back for you. Until I do, you have to watch out for Ed and Mary." He knew he should give her some course of action to take if he should fail to return, but he couldn't bring himself to say it.

Michelle reached up and pulled Davis' lips to her own. "Don't you let anything happen. Please, don't." Then she was crying, only lightly, and Davis disengaged and went back up the stairs long enough to lead the other two down. When all three were sitting together in a bare spot on the floor, he went back out into the town.

Out in the open, in the growing storm, Davis dug about in the rubble, searching. In a little while, he found what he was hunting for and pulled it free of the trash and the dirt. He held the leather section up to the fading light and gazed at the sign drawn on it: the blood sign he had seen floating above, dancing, drawing out the beast. "You bastard. Come out and fight."

Turning, he went to the wagon and pulled away from the square.

Slowly, if somewhat noisily, Davis took the ailing wagon back down the street to where Ed and Mary's house still stood. He crept, searching the forest's periphery for some sign of the thing. In his lap, he kept his right hand on the twelve gauge, steering with his left. Nothing moved. Nothing seemed amiss. He would have thought that it was just another evening. Along the way, he saw that Elvin Hoffman's house was gone, a collection of whitewashed trash and little else. Who had seen? Why weren't the others leaving, trying to get out by way of the logging roads? He doubted that the ones who hadn't seen would believe what had happened. Why should they?

Damn. Now, he was truly beginning to feel foolish. The thing was nowhere. Perhaps it had fled, for whatever reason. He probably could be halfway to the interstate by now, and Michelle would be safely on her way to Martens...

He felt the earthy shuddering even from where he sat in the wagon. Davis stopped the car and got out, feeling the security of the motor humming, knowing it was there for him if he needed it, trying not to think of the mashed remains of Wesley Jarman's pickup. There it was again; he felt it. The vibration was followed by a crashing of small trees underfoot. A motion caught his eye.

Less than a hundred yards away, Davis could see something twisting in the air above Linda Farrell's house. That damned sign that called the thing to feast. He watched it twirling, dancing and slowly coming down toward the ranch-style building. Climbing back into the car, he gunned it and brought the car up to Mrs. Farrell's house. After a moment, he poked his head out of the window and looked up--a similar thing was forming over the wagon.

Davis looked up the street and down. Nothing else moved. No other house was so marked. Sitting there, waiting, he wondered what activated them, what made the sign to form and dance above the monster's victims. Perhaps...

The slashing wind had almost covered the monster's approach.

If it had weighed a ton or two less, maybe it would have actually burst out of the forest without warning. As it was, Davis heard the gigantic treading in time to look and see from where it was coming. The woods across the street from Linda Farrell's house spit it out, the thing striding out and away from the trees like a bit of Earth itself come to life. For some reason, it seemed intent on the woman's house, and chose to aim itself in that direction. In a single step, it crossed the pavement and was thudding atop her lawn, bearing down on the house.

There was a single report, the shotgun bucked in Davis' grasp. The solid slug was aimed true, smacking home against the thick armor plates above its distended gut. The monster made a choking sound, drew up and reassessed its targets.

From up high, from a position taller than many of the pines in which it had recently stalked, the beast regarded the prey it had come to claim. Reptile eyes glittered in what remained of the day, swiveling as they peered down. The prey had struck back; pain registered in its small brain, and blood trickled down from the broken spot in its armor. It dipped its head to examine the wound, and for that motion was rewarded with another blow, this one striking hard on the ridges of scales that made a protective covering above its left eye.

Davis had taken advantage of the beast's momentary confusion to fire again. He could watch as the slug penetrated the fleshy pad on its skull, hoping that it would penetrate to the brain beneath. But the slug merely skimmed along the thick bone there.

Davis saw a splash of red as the slug exited, tearing through the rugged skin at a spot about a foot from where it had entered. The beast roared and turned from the Farrell house.

Just before the taloned foot could come down atop the hood of the wagon, the car rocked forward, away from the impact. Pavement buckled beneath the weight of the monster as Davis swerved to the left and took the car onto someone's yard. Rain was beginning to fall, and he even noticed the first dollops splatting against his windshield. The thing was moving to cut him off, so Davis floored the pedal, surging forward and away from the monster, leaving wet dark lines in the grass for his trouble.

Defying gravity, the beast darted ahead, intending to overtake Davis. He swerved again, jumped a shallow ditch and his tires hummed atop gravel and asphalt. He gained on the thing, although it continued to chase him. Davis smiled, keeping his eye on the unbelievable sight that gritted death at him.

"Follow me, you son-of-a-bitch."

It did.

In their safe place beneath the ruin of the square, Michelle and the Childress couple did not hear the rattling of Kiser's wagon as Davis raced past. Through the slashing of the wind, they did notice the vibrations in the earth as the monster thudded by, crossing over the spot in which Davis had hidden them. They huddled together and watched as rain slowly began to trickle down the stairwell.

During the chase, Davis actually worried that he was going to lose the thing, that it would give up and leave him for easier marks. But he had apparently hurt it, angering it beyond whatever capacity it had for reasoning. It followed, and he took advantage of his greater speed to place some quarter mile between it and him. He would need that quarter of a mile if he were to take the thing with him to where he wanted it to go. Along the way, it would have more than one chance to take shortcuts through the pine while he detoured around lazy curves in the spur road. He could only hope that the quarter mile lead would serve him.

The blood sign that had spun above the car had descended, was directly in his line of sight when Davis came upon the first turn in the route he was taking. Almost, he did not take it in time, the tires screaming on the hard, uneven surface, leaving thin black clouds that were quickly buried by the building rainfall. As Davis straightened up the wheel, he switched on his headlights and took the car down the unpaved road that once led down to the Wishon farm. Where it had all begun for him. "Poor Billy."

The wagon clattered over washboard. "Poor Shelly." Behind him, the monster roared. It was closer; he could see it, its great head pointed at him like God's accusing finger.

To his right, he barely noticed the turn that would take him to where he wanted to be. In the growing gloom, it was barely more than a pale track, a break in the wall of trees. He spun the wheel, jerking it hard. Wet sand flew up, into the palmetto that lined the road. The wagon held onto the sandy path and he barreled onward. Small trees broke like dry twigs as the beast plowed through them, arrowing after the prey that fought back. The thing was on him, less than two hundred feet now separated the pair.

Feeling the thunder of its approach, Davis pressed down, switching on the high beams and illuminated his destination.

Galvanized chain link surrounded the substation with an eight foot wall topped out with triple strands of barbed wire. He knew the gate would be locked, but he didn't have time for gates, anyway.

Although he really couldn't force it any further down, Davis pressed harder on the gas pedal and the grill of the wagon met the chain link gate. The gate snapped wide, smashing backward and forward again, actually catching the auto as if the jaws of some giant insect before they flew back once again.

Davis almost found himself unable to turn the vehicle aside in time, thereby doing to himself what he was hoping to do to the thing bearing down on him. With what remained of his strength, he pulled down on the steering wheel and veered aside enough so that he was able to circle around to the far side of the small station, scattering the crushed granite that carpeted the area on which the power facility was built. Once on the far side, Davis slammed on his brakes, sending a wave of granite chips before him. He heard them clattering down, spinning off into the wind-whipped palmettoes and bear grass. Leaving the car running, he opened the door and rolled free of it, falling face down into the hard gravel, covering his ears, waiting for the huge beast to impact with the substation.

The ground shook, shook, shook. Davis winced, waiting for the flash, for the electric explosion that would take place when the thing came in contact with the raw power surging through the substation.

Nothing happened. The thundering ceased. Davis looked up from where he crouched like a small animal.

On the far side of the metal and ceramics, through the chain link and the wires, the beast stood and surveyed the situation. It had drawn up, stopping just short of collision. Davis wouldn't have believed it, that something so massive and moving at such speed could have stopped so suddenly, so completely. But it had. Its breath came in long, laborious intervals.

The little man could hear its breathing even above the now howling wind, above the slash of the pelting rain. He watched it eyeing him through the mesh of metal.

"Come on, you son-of-a-bitch! Come on and get me! Here I am, goddamit! I'm food, you stupid animal!"

The thing snuffed, as if sucking his tiny human rants through its ham-sized nostrils. And then, and then it leaped, covering half the distance between itself and Ryan in a movement so quick that Davis almost did not see it.

"God! Oh, God!" Davis lifted himself up, still gripping the shotgun in his right hand, and he, too, dodged aside. The thing stood and watched him moving on the periphery of the substation. Davis eyed the steel against which he moved, taking care not to touch, for he knew that even the secondaries were carrying better than 2,000 kilowatts. He limped along on his bleeding feet, placing himself on the far side of the wagon. The thing did not follow him. If only it would try to grab him, he knew it would make contact at some point and all Hell would break loose. It stood, unmoving, unsure of what it had come up against, unable to understand the strange fields being given off by the metal and the power surging through it.

"Damn you, then!" Davis knew there was nothing else to do but take a last chance. Even if it worked, he'd more than likely go with the monster. He thought about poor, small Addie Lacher, and he could do no less. Holding the gun carefully to him, he eased into the array. When he was there, standing amidst the surging power of 200,000 kilowatts, he went to his knee, took careful aim.

Davis realized that one of the secondaries could arc, making contact with the gun he held, and then it would all be over for him, and for everyone else in Woodvine. And who knew what would happen after that. This storm, what Addie had said. He gazed down the barrel at the giant reptile's gut and pulled the trigger.

As weak as Davis was, the recoil actually knocked him back, so that he did not see the slug slam into the small chink in the thing's plated gut. There was a gout of blood, and while the wound was nothing like a mortal one, there was enough pain so that it reacted with a roar unlike any it had ever made. Davis felt as if the sound of it was forcing him down, pressing his shoulders into the angled surface beneath him. And then it leaped, its gigantic bird feet coiled back to trample, its head tucked between them, downward to slash with its dagger teeth at the little meat that stung it.

Fifteen feet above the ground, ten feet into the path it had chosen to leap, its ankle made a terse contact with one of the step-down secondaries. The great spark that angled out illuminated the dark area, and Davis watched as the huge beast went down, its thick tail lashing, the rock garden flesh on its flanks bubbling like Paul Bunyan's cookout. It fell, hitting the ground with a force that seemed to rock the teeth in Ryan's own skull.

Roaring, it got up.

Davis could not believe it. He could not believe that anything, no matter what its size, could have survived what the huge animal had just gone through. But it had. In complete disbelief, he watched as it drew itself up, more slowly than before, eyed him with a gaze that seemed to freeze him to the bone. Again, soundlessly, it leaped.

Davis could see that this time it was not leaping to slash, to try to pick him out of the briar patch, but that it wanted nothing more than to squash him like the bothersome insect he was.

If he remained frozen was, he would die whether the thing came down on him or whether he was crushed by a falling metal column. Careless of where he was going or what was in his way, Davis stood and drove to his left, moving his old feet over the broken rock.

There seemed to be a moment in which nothing moved. As if the wind had stopped and the rain had halted in mid-fall. There was nothing: no rush of blood in his ears, no rasp of breath in his throat, no pounding in his chest. In that moment, he ducked his head, recalling tumbling lessons he had had when he was a small child. The old man somersaulted clumsily free of the perimeter of the substation. The giant thing hunting him came down on it.

Four primaries touched it--on the thick flesh of its tail, on the callused padding of its right foot, against the very spot

Ryan's slug had slapped home, and one rammed into its wide opened maw, meeting the softness of its tongue, frying it like an egg on a griddle. 50,000 kilowatts of power lit up the air above the substation.

Davis watched as the thing landed amidst the tangle of metal and snapping wire. Electricity snarled angrily at the mass that had interrupted its journey.

The thing died.

CHAPTER THIRTY-ONE

"I swear to God, Alec!" He turned to the other lineman and scowled. "I have never seen a mess like this one. These locals can cook up a new way to vandalize our property every time I turn around!"

The Georgia Power truck was parked where the sub-station was supposed to be. The concrete slab was still there, and a melted mass of slag and shattered steel and aluminum and chain link indicated where once there had been a very expensive structure. Now, all the pair could see was a lot of work that would need to be done, a bunch of men who would need to be called in to do it, and a great pile of money that would have to be expended to pay for it all.

Alec leaned forward in his seat as Warren stared in hatred at vandals he could not see but imagined. Warren's imaginary boot was up the ass of each of those destructive sons of bitches. "Fuck if they haven't made the ultimate mess with this one," Alec said. "I reckon this one would qualify as terrorism. That's by God what I think," said, with emphasis. "Goddamn terrorism is what it is."

Together, the pair climbed out of the big two-ton bucket truck. They'd come prepared for trouble, but nothing like this. One truck and a load of tools and a pair of linemen were not going to go anywhere near making this right.

"We'd better phone this one in right now," Alec said to his partner. He was already wearing his full gear—waterproof and insulated against power surges. Like a big, plodding bear the man splashed down in the seeping puddles all around the former sub-station and surveyed the problems that faced the two.

"We'll have to dig out the satellite phone," Warren reminded him. "There's no cell service out here. Or we can drive on into Woodvine and ask to use a land line if that's not out." He eyed the telephone poles that led up and down the roadway, looking to see if any of them were down.

"Hell," he said. "We might get lucky and run into someone who can tell us what went on and who did this."

"I freaking well doubt it," Alec responded. "Whoever did this is probably one mean sumbitch. If the local know who it is, then they're probably going to be too scared to talk about it."

"Well, we'd better get on the horn and notify them what we're up against and what it's going to take to get this station operational again." Warren stood there, hands on his hips, surveying the utterly devastated unit. "I swear to God I didn't see no worse in Iraq."

When everyone began comparing notes, they all realized that it was the power company men who were the first on the scene. They got there before the police, before the ambulances, before even the reporters and the lawyers. They all arrived eventually, but it was the men who'd come to investigate the power outages who got there first.

"What the Hell did this?" That was the questions they kept asking. The sub-station was a wreck. The chain-link barriers around it were shredded, and the framework was in a shambles. It was obvious a great weight had been pressed against the structure, but evidence of the source of that weight seemed to be missing.

Since Davis Ryan was the owner of the vehicle found at the site, he was tracked down and brought back to the location for questioning.

"I don't know," was all that he could tell them. Or, perhaps, it was all that he would tell them. The men from Georgia Power were a suspicious lot, but even they could fathom no reason that a retired former employee would sabotage the sub-station. None of it made any sense.

What especially made no sense was the vast amount of slimy material that coated the Georgia Power property. It wasn't oil, exactly, but it was oily in texture and it smelled something like raw oil. Some samples were taken and sent out to be analyzed, but it never occurred to anyone to test for DNA. It was figured for some kind of chemical compound and the remaining samples were stored away and largely forgotten.

Sheriff Watts was the next in line to roll in. Later, Davis Ryan had laughed how the lawman had seemed to take a back seat to the boys from the power company. The man had seemed to stand aside for them as they went about their business, investigating what property had been damaged, how much work they had to do, and how quickly they could restore power to so many homes.

But the man had finally gotten his minutes alone with everyone he wished to question, and with everyone to whom he figured he should apologize.

The apologies went out, of course, to almost everyone left in Woodvine. When the count was finally done, the population was twenty less than it had been before Davis Ryan had gone calling on the good folk of Martinsville for help.

Sitting at the dining room table in Michelle's house. They'd made him wait a week before agreeing to speak with him. The two had left the county in something of a hurry. They'd gotten married and didn't want to waste another second. Now they were living in the Mrs.' House and Sheriff Watts had his Q & A with the one man in Woodvine who likely had the biggest bone to pick with him.

Elections would be coming up too soon to consider, and Watts figured he'd best patch as many holes in the dike as he could before the leaks become too much.

"You want more tea?" Michelle asked the policeman. Even she could tell that he was nervous and not at all at ease, despite the fact that she had done her best to make him feel at home.

"No ma'am," he told her. "This will be fine for me," he insisted. His eyes glided about the living room, settling now and again on a chair, on a framed photograph, a lamp, a candy dish, this or that. She could almost see the sweat forming at his collar.

Davis Ryan was about to speak up when Sheriff Watts spoke first.

"Look," he told them. "I've come out here to apologize. You went to me for help and I didn't do all I was supposed to do." His words faded and he was searching for some way to say it, for some phrase that could ease his guilt and yet leave him with some honor.

His eyes met Ryan's and locked there. "You are a serious man and I should have seen that when you came to me about this trouble. It's like you said. If I was the kind of sheriff that Harrison was in his day then I'd have known that about you. I should have known your reputation and that you weren't…

"Well, I should have known that you were on the level when you came to tell me about the trouble with the Wishons." Watts swallowed and tried to clear his throat. He seemed to have forgotten that he had half a glass of iced tea and suddenly brought it to his lips to take a long sip. It helped.

"If you're looking to be forgiven, Sheriff Watts, then it's yours. I don't feel any ill toward you. I know you did what you thought was right." Davis felt Michelle's hand on his own and he looked up at her and smiled. He was done with the bad and wanted nothing more than to live out the rest of his life with as much of peacefulness and happiness as he could seek.

"Thank you," he said to Davis, and rose to stride across the room to meet the other man. He extended his hand and Ryan took it. "I don't deserve it, but thanks all the same."

For a few seconds the sheriff stood and moved clumsily about the room, returning to his seat. He wanted to leave, but knew that he had to say a few more things before he could justify moving on.

"We're still hunting for those missing," he said. "We'll keep looking until…" He paused. He wanted to say *until we find them*. But he knew he couldn't say that, because somehow he knew that they'd never find the missing old folk. "Well, we'll keep looking as long as we can."

Finally, it was David Ryan who stood, patting his Michelle on her shoulders, looking down at her with an expression of benevolence. "Look, Sheriff Watts. We all know that you can't search forever. There's no telling where they went and there's no telling where they…well, where they ended up.

"That was a terrible storm that swept through here. If the bodies of the missing were washed away—well, they could be anywhere by now. The Suwannee could have taken them on downriver. They might be in the Okefenokee Swamp for all we'll ever know, or down to the Gulf.

"There's just no way to know, and all we can do is pray." At that, he reached out and put his hand on the law man's shoulder.

Watts stood, and allowed himself to be shepherded to the door and politely out of the house.

Together, the three stood for a moment on Michelle's front porch. In the darkness dispelled just a bit by a single bulb burning on that porch, Davis Ryan pointed out into the encroaching forest all around them. "Listen," he said.

"What is it?" Watts asked, cocking his head to try to figure out what the other man was indicating.

"The bugs are calling. Everything is the way it should be," Ryan finished.

"Eh. Yes, I guess it is," their visitor said, some confusion obvious on his face.

They said their goodbyes and the officer climbed into his car and was soon gone. Davis and Michelle retreated to their home, closed the door, and went to bed.

CHAPTER THIRTY-TWO

Five years passed like breezes through a pine bough.

Woodvine recovered. Against all odds, the little community found itself growing again.

Addie Lacher had deeded what ended up being almost one thousand acres of land to the AME Zion Church in Martinsville. It was to reward them for the years that church had looked out for an old woman sitting alone in the midst of the forest. Her pastor had turned out to be quite the businessman and those acres had thereafter been carved up and turned into a subdivision.

It seemed that Addie's land was good for northern retirees looking for Florida, but who were willing to settle for a plot of land in Georgia just north of the Florida border. Woodvine grew.

In short order the houses began to go up and tenants moved in. Older homes that had sat vacant in town were sold and more families returned. Children's voices were suddenly heard on the breezes of Woodvine once again. And that, in turn, led to the grammar schools being renovated and reopened.

Before almost anyone had noticed, the people who owned the deeds to the old storefronts were contacted and enterprising people had them reopened. Months later there were businesses once again in the village. Restaurants filled the air with the smell of cooking food. Lights went on in long-vacant shops and once more there was a reason to head to the old merchant sector. Grocery stores opened their doors. And a Honda dealership took over the rusted remains of the Chevrolet lot. It wasn't quite the same, but almost.

Davis and Michelle continued their lives. Together, in later days. Their lives were happy and quite normal and without any negative event.

But, sometimes, on certain days, Davis Ryan would pick up the phone and call Pat Wilson.

"Pat," he'd say. "Let's get the boat and head out down Fanner's Creek. I think we need to check."

And, under the soft cover of a white lie of a fishing trip, they'd unload Wilson's fifteen-foot johnboat and head out on that blackwater river. They would have their fishing gear, but unseen by everyone else the two friends would also pack good rifles, and together they'd hunt.

But it wasn't deer, or feral pigs, or rabbits, or squirrels, or turkey, or anything of that sort that they'd search for.

They'd ply those dark waters looking for something else with the rifles loaded for big game.

Because sometimes one of the new locals would make mention of seeing something. They'd claim to have caught a glimpse of something strange in the swampy backwaters or at the lazy bend in Fanners Creek. And it wouldn't be an alligator that they'd seen. It was always something else…something not quite right. A long, sleek body cutting the water. Something with smooth skin nothing like that of a gator, and a triangular head world's different from a crocodilian. It was at such times that Davis and Pat knew they had something to do.

And most of the time they'd spot nothing at all. Most of the time they just cruise the creeks and swamps with the motor running or maybe just paddling along silently, using the oars from time to time, sipping beer and searching. They almost never saw anything worth seeing and would just return to the boat launch in the evening and head for home.

But, sometimes, rarely, they would see exactly what had been described to them. They'd spot a big creature with slick, green skin; a head like a vast triangle with bulging eyes and tremendous jaw muscles indicating amazing power. And at such times they'd move quickly and aim and fire and continue to shoot those rifles until the thing was dead.

Then they'd drag it ashore—all twelve feet of it—and gut it until they were certain it harbored no eggs, no embryonic forms, and then they'd weight it down and sink it to the lowest depths of Fanners Creek.

They were old men and getting older. But so far, so good.

THE END.

ICE STATION ZOMBIE
JE GURLEY

For most of the long, cold winter, Antarctica is a frozen wasteland. Now, the ice is melting and the zombies are thawing. Arctic explorers Val Marino and Elliot Anson race against time and death to reach Australia, but the Demise has preceded them and zombies stalk the streets of Adelaide and Coober Pedy.

www.severedpress.com

The Coalition

When the dead rose to destroy the living, Ron Cutter learned to survive. While so many others died, he thrived. His life is a constant battle against the living dead. As he casts his own bullets and packs his shotgun shells, his humanity slowly melts away.

Then he encounters a lost boy and a woman searching for a place of refuge. Can they help him recover the emotions he set aside to live? And if he does recover them, will those feelings be an asset in his struggles, or a danger to him?

THE STATE OF EXTINCTION: the first installment in the **COALITON OF THE LIVING** trilogy of Mankind's battle against the plague of the Living Dead. As recounted by author **Robert Mathis Kurtz.**

www.severedpress.com

MACHINES OF THE DEAD

The dead are rising. The island of Manhattan is quarantined. Helicopters guard the airways while gunships patrol the waters. Bridges and tunnels are closed off. Anyone trying to leave is shot on sight.

For Jack Warren, survival is out of his hands when a group of armed military men kidnap him and his infected wife from their apartment and bring them to a bunker five stories below the city.

There, Jack learns a terrible truth and the reason why the dead have risen. With the help of a few others, he must find a way to escape the bunker and make it out of the city alive.

www.severedpress.com

JUDGMENT DAY

Dr. Jebediah Stone never believed in zombies until he had to shoot one. Now they're mutating into a new species, capable of reproducing, and the only defence is 'Blue Juice', a vaccine distilled from the blood of rare individuals immune to the zombie plague. Dr. Stone's missing wife is one of these unwilling 'munies', snatched by the military under the Judgment Day Protocol.It's a new, dangerous world filled with zombies, street gangs, and merciless Hunters desperate for a shot of blue juice. Has the world turned on mankind? Is Mortuus Venator the new ruler of earth?

www.severedpress.com

TIMOTHY
MARK TUFO

Timothy was not a good man in life and being undead did little to improve his disposition. Find out what a man trapped in his own mind will do to survive when he wakes up to find himself a zombie controlled by a self-aware virus.

www.severedpress.com

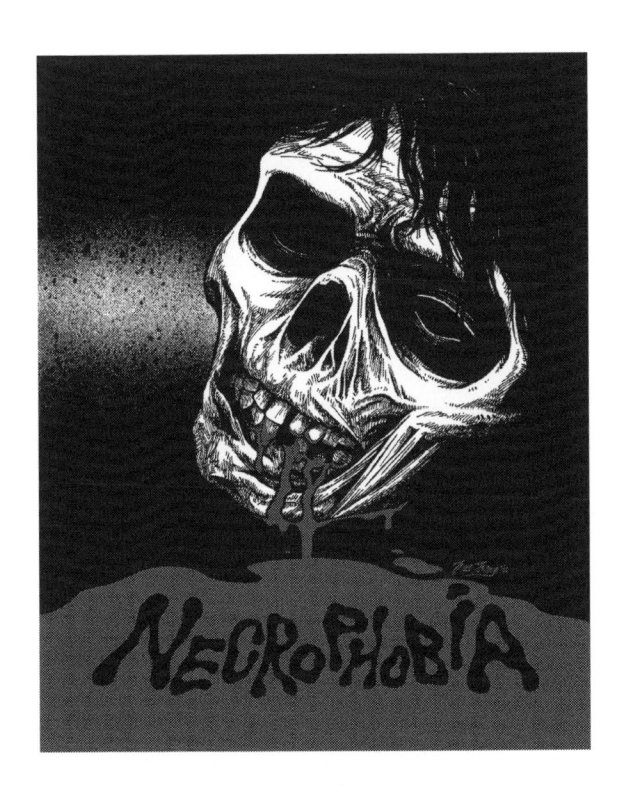

NECROPHOBIA

An ordinary summer's day.
The grass is green, the flowers are blooming. All is right with the world. Then the dead start rising. From cemetery and mortuary, funeral home and morgue, they flood into the streets until every town and city is infested with walking corpses, blank-eyed eating machines that exist to take down the living.
The world is a graveyard.
And when you have a family to protect, it's more than survival.
It's war.

www.severedpress.com

Printed in Poland
by Amazon Fulfillment
Poland Sp. z o.o., Wrocław